THE LOST

THE LOST

TALES OF THE ABLOCKALYPSE
BOOK TWO

DAVID H. SCOTT

PUBLISHED BY MYSTIC AWESOME PRESS

ISBN-13: 978-0-9949221-1-3
ISBN-10: 0-9949221-1-3
Ebook: 978-0-9949221-2-0

Printed in the United States of America

To my cousin Shaun,
who introduced me
to the wonderful game of
Minecraft®

CHAPTER 1

S teve felt for a foothold on the rocky cliff. He really did not want to look down. He wasn't sure how high he was, but he knew if he slipped and fell, death would certainly await him. His muscles ached from the strain of climbing. Looking up he saw that he was still a long way from the top. He was beginning to worry he wouldn't make it.

His foot found a hold, and he pushed himself up enough to grasp at a crag in the cliff-face with his hand. Painfully, he pulled himself a few inches higher.

He found another foothold and put his weight on it. He felt the ground slip beneath him. He grasped at the cliff with his free hand, finding nothing but loose dirt and air. Dangling by only one hand, Steve forced himself not to panic. He searched with his feet for a foothold, and quickly found one that would support his weight.

Relief flooded through him. Looking around for his next handhold, he saw something from his new position. It looked like a small cave in the cliff to the right of him.

"I just need to make it there, I can rest for a while," Steve muttered to himself. He figured his chances of surviving the climb would increase a lot if he could just rest his weary arms. That thought gave him both renewed hope and a spurt of energy. He focused on finding the easiest path to the opening.

As he neared the cave entrance, he realized that changing direction might have been a critical mistake. He heard the sounds of skeleton warriors below, searching the face of the cliff for him. They spotted him before he reached the cave, and the first arrows began shattering rocks nearby. He quickened his pace, spending less time testing crevices and footholds as he scrambled to get to the entrance before one of the arrows found its mark. Just as he finally grasped the ledge that would lead him to safety, an arrow struck just inches from his face. Shards of rock flew into his eyes, blinding him as he heaved himself into the hollow.

Still blind and trying to rub the debris from his eyes, he stood up. Another arrow whizzed by, grazing Steve's shoulder. He whirled around, disturbing a colony of bats that had been roosting on the roof of the cavern. They flew by Steve, knocking him off balance. He swung his arms wildly and scrambled toward the wall. He realized a moment too late that he'd been turned around and what he had thought was wall was empty space. He stepped into nothingness and felt his body plummet to the earth.

Chapter 2

Steve woke up flailing, his mind believing he was about to meet the ground in a deadly crash. His entire body shook.

"Wake up, dude!" After a moment, he opened his eyes and his head cleared. His friend Clem was shaking him by his shoulders. "It's your shift. Time to hunt some monsters!"

Steve rolled out of bed and rubbed his eyes. "One of these days I'm going to need a full night's sleep, you know." He grabbed his diamond chest-plate and threw it on over his crumpled shirt.

"You were having one heck of a dream," Clem commented as he watched Steve prepare for the nightly battle.

"Nightmare. It's the first one I've had since getting back," Steve told him. "I used to have them all the time. I thought they might be gone. Roger said they'd stop."

In fact, Roger, the villager who had sent him on

his first quest, had lied about a lot of things. He'd sent Steve off to stop the coming Ablockalypse, and he promised that completing the quest would cure him of his nightmares. Both of those things had proved to be completely false.

Steve nudged his dog with his foot. "C'mon Chopper. Time to fight monsters." Chopper whimpered, and blearily opened one eye. He was not a morning canine.

"You should get some sleep now, Clem. I'll see you when the sun comes up."

Clem nodded and turned to go to the guest bedroom. "I set out some food for you. You'll need your energy if you want to last the rest of the night."

"Thanks, man," Steve said gratefully. "Sleep well."

Steve smiled as he looked at the meal set out for him in the kitchen. Clem was a mercenary by trade, but you'd never guess his occupation from his unfailing cheerfulness and easy-going manner, not to mention his usual uniform, which consisted of scruffy jeans and tie-dyed t-shirts.

Clem had been staying with Steve since they'd returned from their last adventure. Together they were planning to go in search of a particular diamond helmet - the third piece to complete Steve's set of enchanted armor - but their quest had stalled due to lack of information. It seemed that no one had any idea where to begin searching for the missing item.

As he and Chopper ate enough food to satisfy their hungry bellies, Steve thought about the community he'd come to love. The monster attacks each night were becoming more and more severe. It was becoming difficult to protect the village. The number of creatures that spawned to attack the village seemed to increase every night. Some villagers that lived on the outskirts of town had already decided to pack up and leave.

Taking a quick look at the time, Steve saw that his shift was about to begin. He popped the last piece of toast in his mouth, grabbed his enchanted sword, and headed out the door with Chopper at his heels.

The moon was bright as he headed toward his post. He and Clem usually took charge of the areas that were most vulnerable to attack -- Clem, because he was the most experienced fighter, and Steve because his diamond chest-plate and sword made him nearly invincible.

When he got to the area where a team of villagers was fighting, he jumped right in and began making short work of the attacking creatures. His sword glinted in the moonlight as he slashed his way through the invaders. Chopper ran to the side and proceeded to attack the zombies that were trying to flank them.

Steve and the group of villagers with him fought steadily until the sun started to peek over the horizon. They found renewed energy once the sun's light shone on them. Knowing that no more monsters would be spawning in the light of day, they made short work of the final attackers.

Steve sat down on a tree stump and took a drink from the flask by his side, waving to his friends and acquaintances as they all shuffled home to get some rest. As he offered some water to his thirsty dog, he noticed Clem running up the lane toward him.

"Dude!" The older man called out. "Hazel's got news!"

Chapter 3

Steve rushed home. He wanted to hear what Hazel had to say, but he knew from experience that it was a bad idea to visit her house straight after fighting. She didn't appreciate the lingering smell of battle, or the monster guts dripping on her floors. Steve quickly washed himself and his weapon and changed into clean clothes. As he entered the kitchen, he saw Clem and Chopper waiting for him.

"So, did Hazel tell you what the news was?" Steve grabbed some bread and meat from the pantry and threw a porkchop to Chopper.

"Sort of. She said she might have found a story that talks about a legend that hints about the location of the armor," Clem paused while he grabbed an extra slice of bread from Steve's plate and took a bite. "It's probably another dead-end, but maybe she found something that's worth checking out."

Before Steve could finish his food, there was a knock at the door. Clem motioned for him to keep eating as he went to answer it. He came back a few moments later with Roger tailing him. "Hey! It's Roger. He wants to know if you want to trade seven emeralds for a wooden shovel!"

Roger grinned at Steve happily. "Don't exaggerate, Clem!" he said. "I only want five emeralds for the spade!"

"I never know if you're serious about these insane trades, or if you're just putting me on," Steve said. "Either way, I don't know what Hazel sees in you."

"Is that a no?" Roger asked.

Clem burst out laughing, and Steve couldn't help but grin. "It's a no, Roger."

Roger grinned back. "I was just on my way back from Hazel's cottage. She asked me to check on the dragon and pick up a potion that she'd been brewing for the past week."

"Can she still do that?" Clem asked, "Brew potions, I mean. Since we lifted the curse, she's not a witch anymore."

"I don't know," said Roger with a shrug, "She thinks she can, but if you ask me, this potion has gone very, very wrong."

He pulled a vial out from his pack and unstopped the cork, letting Steve and Clem smell the concoction. Steve's eyes watered and Clem reeled back, gagging. Roger put the cork back in and smiled, "See what I mean?"

Neither Steve nor Clem answered him. Both of them were desperately trying to keep the contents of their stomachs from violently leaving their bodies. Roger gave them a moment to compose themselves before he asked, "Are you heading to our place now? Hazel is anxious to show you what she found last night."

"Yeah. We were just about to leave," Clem said. "So, how's Ruby? She and I did a lot of test flights yesterday; I hope I didn't wear her out."

"The dragon is fine," Roger said. "I don't know why you're so obsessed with making the perfect saddle."

"That's because you never tried to ride her bare-back," Clem snorted.

Steve nodded in agreement. They had rescued and befriended the extremely large, impossibly red dragon on their last adventure. Their hasty escape on her back had stuck in his memory as one of the worst experiences of his life. Clem's attempts to make future dragon flights more comfortable for them was much appreciated.

Steve popped the last bit of food into his mouth and said, "C'mon, let's see what Hazel's got for us."

Chapter 4

Hazel and Roger's house looked like a tornado had hit it, but only on the inside. Roger's stuff was strewn about the floor and on all the furniture. Hazel had cleaned up a small part of the kitchen so she could work on her research.

Steve, Clem, and Roger picked their way through the mess. "Don't you ever clean up after yourself, Roger?" Steve asked, "This place isn't suitable for human life!"

Roger looked at him petulantly. "Bugging me about cleaning is Hazel's job, not yours."

Hazel looked up from the book she was studying, "Go ahead and nag him, Steve. I've been pestering him for days to start picking up his dirty clothes," she said. "It's driving me nuts!"

Clem headed over to the kitchen table. "What have you got for us?"

Hazel pointed to a page in the book she had open in front of her. "Look at this."

They all gathered round and looked at the pages of the book she was pointing out. "Um, I hate to sound like the only idiot here," Steve said. "But I have no idea what I'm looking at. I don't even recognize the language!"

Hazel smiled. "I was so immersed in my research that I forgot it was written in the ancient tongue."

"So, what does it say?" Clem asked.

"It's an ancient legend about the forging of the enchanted armor," Hazel explained. "It tells the story of a time when dragons were a large and powerful race that had lived in peace with men. Together, the two races forged the enchanted armor to fight off the dangerous monsters that were plaguing the land."

She turned the page and continued, "Dragons and people lived peacefully together until the armor fell into the hands of an evil man. He was jealous of the power and strength of the dragon race, and with the enchanted items under his control, he decided to eradicate dragons from the world."

"The dragons, being peaceful creatures, tried to reason with him and his followers, but were killed by the hundreds for their efforts. Finally, they came up with a plan to get the armor and sword back. They managed to regain control of the three items, although it cost many dragon lives. The sword, helmet, and chest plate were separated, with each hidden in a different secret location so that no one would ever be able to use their combined power again."

"Well, that doesn't seem to have worked out quite

as well as they hoped," Steve said, "since I've got two of the three pieces already."

"Does the manuscript have some sort of idea what will happen when the pieces are reunited? There's always a story about a chosen one who saves the world in these stories," Roger said hopefully.

Steve glared at him. "Don't think I haven't forgotten about your little lie about me being the chosen one."

Hazel raised her hand to silence the squabbling as she interrupted. "The dragons didn't seem to have considered the possibility that all three pieces could ever be found."

"Maybe they shouldn't be found," Clem said. "Maybe we should forget about searching for the helmet."

Hazel shook her head, "I've thought about that, and I don't have much in the way of evidence, but I do feel that we need to reunite the armor if we want to see an end to the growing wave of evil."

"I trust your hunches," Clem shrugged. "So, what do we do?"

Hazel looked up and said, "You're going to have to find the enchanted helmet, and to do that, you're going to have to talk to a dragon."

Clem looked at Hazel like she had lost her mind. "Hazel, dear, I think you've been breathing the fumes from your potions for too long. Dragons don't talk!"

Chapter 5

"You're right. Dragons don't talk the same way we do," Hazel explained. "But they do have ways to communicate. Steve, you must have noticed that Ruby understands what you want her to do."

"Yeah, at least some of the time," Steve replied. "And she and Chopper seem to be able to communicate too."

Hazel pointed to an illustration in her book that showed a man with a strange hat apparently speaking with a dragon. "This," she said, "is a Dragon Master."

"What's that?" Clem asked.

"Throughout history, there has always been one man chosen to learn the secrets of communicating with dragons," Hazel said. "The last recorded Dragon Master lived a long time ago, but there is a chance he trained a replacement, who trained another replacement, which means that there is a chance, however slim, that there is still a Dragon Master living today."

"You've got to be kidding!" Steve exclaimed. "Why

would someone even want to learn how to talk to dragons when everyone believes that the Ender Dragon is the only one in existence! I doubt that creature has many kind things to say to anyone!"

"Nevertheless," Hazel replied, "this manuscript seems to indicate that the masters believed that the dragon race would rise again in the future. If that belief was passed on, then maybe there's a chance the skills were as well."

"Ok," Clem said. "So, where would we find this dragon-talker?"

Hazel flipped the book to a map and pointed. Steve and Clem both leaned over to look. "This is the border between what was traditionally dragon land and human land." She ran her finger down a thin line on the map. "My guess would be that the Dragon Master would live somewhere along this line."

"So, we now have a place to start looking!" Steve said. "When should we go?"

"We have enough iron and snow golems to keep the village safe for three nights," Hazel said. "It's still pretty early in the morning, so if you head out now, you'll be able to start your search of the area before nightfall."

"Just be back before three days are up," Roger said, "Or the village will be overrun with monsters!"

Clem stood up, "Then we should pack some stuff and get going,"

"I've already got that covered," Hazel said. She pointed to some bags in the corner of the room. "There's food, supplies, and even some extra clothes in there for you. You'll just need to grab your weapons and armor from home, and you can be off."

Steve began to rise, but Hazel grabbed his arm. "Before you go, I have one more thing for you." She took the vial of potion that Roger had brought with him and poured it into a bowl. Steve nearly passed out from the smell.

Hazel then took a map, and immersed it into the smelly liquid, then put Steve's hand in the mixture as well.

"Ewwwww!" Steve exclaimed. "That's incredibly disgusting!" Steve pulled out his hand, and Hazel passed him a cloth as she pulled out the map and began wiping it off.

Steve cleaned off his hand and smelled it. "It still stinks," he whined. "What did you do that for?"

Hazel held up the now clean map and pointed to a dot on the paper. "That's you. Wherever you are, that dot will move with you. With this map, you'll be able to see where you are, even when you're flying above the clouds."

"Whoa! That's cool!" said Clem.

"Great," Steve said sullenly, glaring at his friend. "But you're not the one with a stinky hand."

CHAPTER 6

It hadn't taken Clem and Steve long to grab their weapons and head over to Hazel's cabin to meet up with Ruby. Once they'd gotten the saddle secured on the enormous red dragon, they climbed aboard and buckled Chopper into the basket that Clem had built for him at the front of the contraption. They waved goodbye to Roger and Hazel, promising to return within three days.

After a bumpy running start, Ruby and her passengers were flying high above the countryside. Steve was amazed at how comfortable the ride was on Clem's new saddle design. Aside from the fast moving air stinging his face, he felt great.

Clem was looking at the map. "This is so cool, Steve! The dot on the page moves in whatever direction we do!" He paused. "Ruby's really flying fast. We're covering a lot of ground."

Steve leaned over and looked at the map as Clem

continued, "At this rate we'll be at the start of the border before dark. We should probably land around here," he pointed to the map. "That way we can walk through the nearby homes while on foot."

"What about Ruby?" Steve asked. "I think she'd freak people out if she were wandering the streets."

"Hopefully, we can let her know that we want to meet her up ahead," Clem replied. "She seems to understand us better than we understand her."

It was early evening when Clem called out to Steve, "Hang on tight. I'm going to get Ruby to land here."

Remembering the last, terrible, horrible, dragon landing he'd experienced, Steve used all the strength he could muster in his hands and legs to grip the dragon. He was surprised to find his efforts weren't necessary. Even though the landing was bumpy, the saddle Clem had designed cushioned and stabilized them very well.

"Wow! Great work, Clem!" Steve exclaimed. "I can't believe how smooth that landing was!"

Clem grinned. "Yeah. I won't tell you how many times I fell off when I was experimenting with design. I'm glad I finally got it right."

They did their best to communicate to Ruby that she should meet up with them at the base of the mountain range that intersected the dragon border in a few days. After a few minutes of mixing words, gestures and emphatic pointing, Steve was pretty sure she'd gotten the message. They shouldered their packs and began walking toward the nearby settlement while Ruby flew off into the clouds.

"Think she'll find the right place?" Steve asked Clem.

"Yep. I'm almost certain she will," Clem replied. "I've been working with her for a while, perfecting the saddle. She's incredibly intelligent. Maybe smarter than you, dude."

"Is that a compliment to Ruby, or an insult to me?"

Clem just laughed in reply as they increased their pace to keep up with Chopper as he bounded ahead.

A few hours later, they caught sight of a village in the distance.

Clem pointed at the rooftops and said, "Let's head to that village and see if there's a tavern or inn. We might be able to gather some information about the dragon talker's location."

Steve looked at him flabbergasted. "We're just going to walk in and ask directions to the Dragon Masters residence? People will think we're crazy!"

"Of course not," Clem said rolling his eyes. "You're clearly in over your head. Let the pro do the talking."

Chapter 7

Once they entered the village, they followed the signs that pointed the way to the nearest tavern. Clem greeted the locals as he and Steve walked in and sat down at the bar.

The bartender wiped the counter, placed two full glasses in front of them, and said "I don't recognize you folks. Are you new in town?"

"We were just passing through, actually," Clem replied.

"Where are you heading?"

"We're meeting a friend at the base of the mountains," Clem said, not mentioning that the friend they were talking about was a red dragon.

"You have a long way to go then," said the bartender.

"Yep, we're just stopping here to get some food, rest for the night, and maybe get a bit of advice," Clem explained. "We've heard of some crazy hermit types living around these parts, and we would like to avoid confrontation with them if at all possible."

The bartender smiled and said, "We've only got one of those around here, but he's the craziest you'll ever meet! He calls himself the Dragon Master, believe it or not. He's always wandering around, picking up stones and calling them his dragon eggs." Pausing for a moment, he added with a smirk, "He probably sits on them at night, trying to hatch them."

Steve's mouth dropped open, and his eyes betrayed his excitement until Clem's elbow painfully made contact with his ribs.

"We certainly wouldn't want to run into him! Would we Steve?"

"No, Clem. I'm sure we wouldn't," Steve muttered through gritted teeth.

"Where does this dragon guy usually wander?" Clem asked the bartender.

The bartender thought for a moment and replied, "He's usually doing his egg hunting on the main road leading to the mountains just out of town." He pulled a map out from under the counter and placed it in front of Clem. Pointing out a thin line leading out of the village, he said, "See this path? It's less traveled and a bit rough, but it runs parallel to the main road for several miles. If you take that route, then redirect to the main path about here," he indicated another location on the map, "You'll get to where you're going and avoid the Dragon Master entirely. It might take you a bit longer, but it will save you from having to deal with our local kook."

Clem studied the map for a moment before handing it back to the bartender with a smile. "Thank you very much. You've helped us more than you know." As an afterthought, he asked, "How is the monster situation around here? Have they been more intense lately here too?"

"It's gotten really bad," said the bartender. "The village has hired a small army to deal with it each night, but if it doesn't let up soon, we're going to run out of money, and then we'll be on our own."

"Sorry to hear that. I hope things improve soon. At least, for now, you're all safe."

Steve and Clem finished off their drinks, and Clem put some money on the counter before they headed out the door.

As they exited the tavern, Chopper came bounding towards them from the shade of a large tree where he'd been resting. Together the three companions headed toward the inn where they would stay overnight.

When Steve was sure no one could hear them, he said, "That was incredible Clem! You got him to tell us exactly what we wanted to know without revealing anything about our plans!"

"Years of experience, dude."

"But," Steve whined as he rubbed his ribcage, "Did you have to hit me so hard back there? That's going to leave a bruise!"

CHAPTER 8

They woke before the sun came up, and were on their way just as the first light of the morning shone over the horizon. They were both amazingly refreshed. Steve realized it was the first full night's sleep they'd had in weeks.

As they walked along the main road, Clem kept wandering off the path to examine rocks. Steve didn't know what he was doing until Clem finally chose one that he was satisfied with, and handed it to Steve.

"Oh, I get it now! It's an egg!" Steve exclaimed.

"Yeah," Clem said. "If this guy really is crazy, it might help to join in the insanity."

"Should we have another one?" Steve asked. "I'll help you look."

For the next several miles, Steve and Clem scoured the roadside for egg-shaped rocks while Chopper bounded between them enjoying the walk in the country. As they found new rocks, they compared them with what they already had found and kept only the ones they thought were the best.

They were so intent on their search that they almost missed the ragged old man wandering the road ahead.

They were almost upon him when Clem finally noticed the stranger, pulling Steve behind a large boulder to hide. "Let's just watch him for a few minutes."

They watched the Dragon Master wander from side to side picking up rocks, examining them and then discarding them, all the while murmuring to himself.

"He's certainly crazy, but he seems harmless enough," Clem whispered to Steve. "Let's circle back and meet up with him, and present the old fellow with our eggs."

Steve nodded, and they silently crept out of their hiding place and circled back to the road where they pretended to be egg hunting just like the old man.

When they came near enough to him, Clem called out, "Hello sir! You wouldn't happen to be the Dragon Master, would you?"

The old man looked at them suspiciously. "Who's asking?"

"My name's Clem, and this is my buddy Steve. We're just out here hunting for dragon eggs. We've heard this is a good place to look for them."

This was apparently the wrong thing to say. The old man charged at them with his cane raised menacingly. "You leave my eggs alone!" he yelled at them as he chased them back down the road. "Mine! They're all mine!"

Clem and Steve retreated quickly. As they ran, Steve called, "You were saying something about him being harmless?"

"I clearly misjudged. Time to change tactics," Clem said. "Go left!"

Steve and Chopper veered to the left while Clem turned to the right. The Dragon Master stopped in the middle of the road, not sure which of them to pursue.

"We're terribly sorry for taking your eggs, sir," Clem called out to the man, who was still waving his cane in the air. "We'd like to give these ones back to you, if you'd just promise not to hit us!"

The old man looked from Clem to Steve, then back to Clem again. He had a short conversation with himself before finally lowering his cane and calling out, "Ok, then. As long as you give me my eggs."

Steve and Clem scrambled back down the road and carefully approached the man. He was dirty, his clothes were ragged, and he smelled suspiciously like a garbage dump.

Clem held out his egg-shaped stone. "Here you go. It's a pretty nice one, isn't it?"

The Dragon Master took the rock, examined it, then tossed it aside. "You idiot. Don't you know an ordinary rock when you see it?"

Clem stifled a laugh and tried to look chastened as the old man grabbed Steve's rock.

"Well, this one is a little closer," the man said. "But you're still an idiot." He tossed that stone away as well.

Steve did his best to look embarrassed while Clem's

shoulders were shaking with laughter. "We're sorry, sir," Steve said. "We thought they looked like dragon eggs, but, to be honest, we've never seen a real dragon egg, so we didn't know what we were looking for."

"Well, of course you've never seen a real dragon egg," the old man said. "It's not like you'd find them laying around on the side of the road!"

Steve was flabbergasted. "Right. I suppose they wouldn't just be lying around. So, um. What are you looking for here by the roadside?"

"Dragon eggs, naturally!"

Steve scratched his head in confusion. "I don't get it," he muttered. He looked over at Clem who was nearly bursting from controlling his laughter. He was shaking, and tears were forming in his eyes. "Clem," Steve implored. "Help me out here!"

Clem wiped his eyes, cleared his throat, and tried to compose himself. "Right, dude," he said to Steve. "Well, I guess because the Dragon Master is an expert, he can search for dragon eggs at the side of the road, where they certainly won't be found," Clem tried to explain, "But being the expert, he's got a far better chance of not finding them than we do."

"Exactly!" said the old man, giving Clem a big toothless grin.

It was Steve's turn to stifle his laughter. Clem's explanation was completely ridiculous, but the Dragon Master was obviously happy about finding a person who understood him.

Clem grinned back at the man and asked, "Do you

think you could give us some pointers on what to look for when we're not finding dragon eggs on the side of the road?"

Chapter 9

It wasn't long before Clem and the Dragon Master were talking as though they were the best of friends, and Clem managed to convince the old man to invite them back to his home. Steve stayed silent as they walked, unable to contribute to a conversation he couldn't follow.

They smelled the Dragon Master's house before they saw it. Like its owner, the house smelled like a neglected garbage dump. Hazel's potions smelled like perfume in comparison. As they got nearer, Steve tried to cover his nose with his shirt to filter out some of the odor.

When the cottage came into view, the Dragon Master seemed surprised to see it. He started jumping up and down, saying, "I live here! I live here!"

Since that was their planned destination, Steve wasn't sure what the old man was excited about, but Clem played right along. "Wow!" the mercenary said.

"Just imagine us running into your house right here in the woods!"

"I know!" said the Dragon Master.

"If you invite us in, we've got some food we can share," Clem said.

"I have a great idea!" the old man exclaimed. "I could invite you guys to come to my house, and you can give me food!"

"What an excellent plan!" Clem said. "Why didn't I think of that?"

Steve's eyes watered as they approached the entrance to the small cabin, but the smell outside was nothing compared to the stench that sent him reeling backward when the door was opened. The interior of the house was in shambles, and it was clear that no one had taken the time to do any cleaning, or even take out the trash, in years.

"I'm never going to complain about Roger being messy again," he said to Chopper. The dog, however, was not there. Chopper had declined to enter the house but instead had chosen to retreat to the shade of a tree upwind from the old man's residence. Steve envied him.

The Dragon Master closed the door behind them as they entered his home. A moment later, without warning, the old man waved his stick menacingly with a crazed look in his eyes.

"Who are you, and what are you doing here?" he shouted. "Why are you in my house?"

Steve reached for his sword, but Clem held him

back. "I'm Clem, and this is my friend Steve," the mercenary calmly said. "You invited us here so we could share our food with you."

"You have food?" Give it to me!"

"How about you sit down here, and I'll go into the kitchen and make us all some lunch," Clem said.

The Dragon Master seemed to calm down at the thought of food. He absent-mindedly wiped a bunch of trash off of what Steve thought was probably a chair and sat down. Steve looked around for a place to sit, but there was nothing in the house that he wanted to touch. He remained standing in the middle of the room as Clem disappeared into what he supposed was a kitchen.

After a while, the silence began to bother Steve. He turned to the Dragon Master, who was sitting cross-legged on his chair rocking back and forth, humming to himself, "So, um, do you have a name? Or should we just keep calling you Dragon Master?"

"Yes! I'm the Dragon Master!"

"Is that your name?"

"Of course not!"

"So what is your name?" Steve persisted.

"It's what my mother called me!"

Steve sighed, "What did your mother call you?"

The old man got up from his chair and started running around the room, "No, Ladon! Sit down! Eat your vegetables! Stop that Ladon! Pay attention! Go to bed, Ladon!"

Steve interrupted the old man's rant. "So, your name

is Ladon?"

The man stopped running, looked Steve squarely in the eye and said, "Maybe."

At that moment, Clem came back into the room carrying a tray of food and drinks. "Sorry it took so long. I had to wash some dishes."

He handed some steak to the Dragon Master, along with a cup of milk. He did the same for Steve before he cleared space on the floor and sat down on the dirty rug.

The Dragon Master sat back down on his chair and dug into his food greedily. After a few bites, he stuck out his tongue, revealing a mouth that was full of food, but nearly empty of teeth. "Tastes funny."

"Probably because it's off of a clean plate," said Clem. "The flavor's always better when it isn't covered with dirt."

"Don't like it," the old man mumbled as he passed out, his face landing on his plate.

Chapter 10

"What did you do to Ladon?" Steve asked Clem accusingly.

"Who's Ladon?"

Steve pointed at the old man.

"He's just sleeping," Clem said with a shrug. "I gave him some of the sleeping potion that Hazel made."

"You carry around a sleeping potion?"

"It was actually for you. I told Hazel you were having nightmares, and she was worried you weren't getting enough sleep."

Steve wasn't sure what to make of that, so he decided to ponder it later and move on to more important matters in the present. "So now you've knocked him out, what's the plan?" He asked Clem.

"It doesn't look like he's going to be much use to us in his current state, so I suggest we search this place for anything that might help - books, papers, diaries, anything that could point us in the right direction."

"Ugh!" Steve said as he looked around. "Where do we even start?"

"Let's start cleaning up. I'm sure once we get the trash out of the way, we'll be able to see what's useful and what's not."

Steve sighed unhappily. "Ok, I guess. I can't believe our adventure has turned into free housecleaning for the completely insane."

Together Steve and Clem worked to remove a decade's worth of trash from the inside of the house. They started with the rotting food, dumping it off the cliff behind Ladon's yard. With the food gone and the windows open, the air in the old shack soon became clear enough that Chopper ventured in to see what they were up to.

It was only after going through several layers of papers that were clearly nonsense that Steve found the first useful thing in the house. "Check this out, Clem! I think this is his diary."

"I've found lots of diaries," Clem said skeptically. "Does this one make any sense?"

"Yeah. This one seems to be from when he was normal. Kind of. He writes a lot about going to the End to see the dragon there."

"Dude! Why would he want to talk to that creature? The thing is pure evil, from what I've heard." Clem said.

"I've heard the same," Steve said. "But I guess if you've trained your whole life to talk to dragons, and there's only one to talk to, you'd want to at least try, no matter how evil the creature is."

Clem shrugged. "Are there any clues about what happened?"

Steve flipped through the pages of the diary "He seemed to be sane up until the day he left. When he came back, however, his entries are filled with angry rants." Steve flipped to the back of the book. "Within a couple of weeks, he was writing the sort of gibberish that we've been finding in his most recent diaries."

"So the encounter with the Ender Dragon was likely what pushed him over the edge," Clem thought out loud. "Are there any clues in there about how to talk to dragons?"

"No, but he mentions some book called *Dragon Mastery*," Steve said. "He apparently owned a copy. We should try and find it."

"Sounds like something that would be useful," Clem said walking toward the bookcase he'd been cleaning earlier. "I wonder if it's in here. I've been sorting the stuff I've found. Diaries are on the bottom and reference books are up here."

He scanned the titles in the bookcase, then grinned as he reached up to grab a thick leather-bound book from the top shelf. "Found it!"

"That's it? Great job, Clem!" Steve said excitedly.

Together they huddled over the thick volume. "Look at this, Clem! It says there are certain artifacts that were crafted by dragons that can help humans communicate with them. We need to find one of those!"

Clem nodded, "Let's keep reading. Maybe the book will give us some clues so we know what the artifacts might be."

They were so absorbed in the book that they didn't realize the sun was going down. Their first hint that night was approaching was a loud banging on the door. Chopper began barking furiously, and Clem and Steve both looked up from the book, simultaneously yelling, "Zombies!"

Steve ran to the door as Clem carefully placed the manuscript in a bag to keep it safe.

By the time Clem reached the entrance to help Steve, several zombies had already been dispatched, but there seemed to be a nearly infinite number of others pressing forward to attack.

Clem drew his sword and stepped beside Steve hacking and slashing at the zombies as they surged towards the door.

After what seemed like hours of fending off monsters Clem hollered to Steve over the noise of battle, "How do you think Ladon fights all these guys off every night?"

Steve had been wondering the same thing. "Dunno!" he called back.

It didn't seem possible that one man, especially not a crazy one, could defend against this sort of attack nightly.

Their host chose that moment to wake from his sleep. Chopper let out a sharp bark to alert them to Ladon's presence. The barking was unnecessary, as the Dragon Master announced himself with a shrill scream. "Visitors! Hooray! I've got visitors!"

Clem and Steve were caught by surprise as Ladon

grabbed his staff and began hitting them with it, yelling, "Stop scaring away my guests!"

Chopper ran to rescue his companions by placing himself between the old man and the zombie fighters. The dog barked excitedly and jumped up, pushing Ladon back further into the room.

Chopper managed to keep Ladon away for only a few moments before the old man's swinging staff struck the dog's body with a sickening thud.

"Chopper!" Steve yelled in alarm as he turned around to help his dog.

Clem grabbed Steve's shoulder and turned him back toward the door. "I'll take care of it, dude," he said.

Steve resumed his fight against the attacking zombies as Clem faced off with Ladon. "Hey, Ladon," he said, "You haven't had visitors before? We're just playing a little game with your new friends."

The Dragon Master lowered his staff and looked at Clem expectantly. "A game? Can I play?"

Clem smiled at the old man, "Of course!" he said. "Come over here, and I'll tell you the rules. Have something to drink while you're listening."

The old man accepted the offered drink and took a sip. A few moments later he fell forward into Clem's waiting arms.

Clem lowered the unconscious Dragon Master into his chair and went to check on Chopper. The dog was tender, but it didn't seem like anything was broken. "Chopper's okay!" Clem shouted as he headed back to the door to help Steve. Together the pair continued fighting off the monsters until the sun began to peek over the horizon.

The Dragon Master was still asleep when the last of the monsters slunk away into the shadows. "Did I hear that right?" Steve asked Clem, "He's never had monsters here before?"

Clem nodded. "That's what he said. I find it a little hard to believe, though."

"Yeah," Steve replied. "The bartender said the village was having monster problems, and tonight sure proved that there are more than a few out here. So how could Ladon never have seen them before?"

"Maybe he forgot. The dude forgot who we were three times on the walk back to his place."

"Maybe," Steve mused, "but can you see him fighting off all the monsters we saw tonight? Every night?"

"Nope. Definitely not."

"But, how could that be?" Steve asked. "Why would the monsters stay away when he's here, then show up at the same time we did? Do you think they're following us? Did we bring them here?"

"Doesn't seem likely," Clem replied. "The village had lots of monster attacks. Maybe the zombies just found this place now."

"You can't be serious!"

"Well, no. Not serious," Clem said with despair in his voice. "What I was thinking, and I hope this isn't true, was that the smell of the place kept the zombies at bay. By cleaning up, we left Ladon vulnerable."

"Oh no." Steve said. "So it is our fault?"

"I think so," Clem said. "But you know what this means, right?"

Steve paused for a moment, then realized what Clem was thinking. "No." Steve shook his head, "No way. Don't say it!"

Clem shrugged apologetically, "We have to take him with us."

CHAPTER 11

While the Dragon Master slept, Clem and Steve rifled through his home, grabbing reference books and anything that looked like it might be an artifact. They were less careful about cleaning up now that they knew they weren't leaving the old man behind. With the monsters now willing to approach the cabin, it wasn't likely that there would be anything left if he ever made it home again.

"You know, we can't take him with us on the quest. He's too unpredictable," Steve said as he threw a bunch of odd-looking gems he found under a chair into his bag.

"I know. We'll head back to the village and drop him off there. Roger and Hazel can look after him. Maybe Hazel can even do something for him."

Steve grinned. "I actually like that thought. Ladon can out-annoy Roger any day. It would be fun to witness them living together."

Clem laughed in agreement as he threw what looked like armbands and necklaces into his bag. "We'll be earlier than expected, but I think that's good. I've been worried about the village's defenses and how they're holding up with us gone."

Ladon was still asleep when they finished searching the house. They bundled up all the books and objects they'd found, and tried to distribute them evenly in their packs.

"We're going to have to wake up the old dude and make him walk with us," Clem said. "It's going to be hard enough lugging all this stuff out of here without carrying him too."

"He's going to freak out about his house," Steve said. "Maybe we should take him a little way down the road before we wake him."

So, the pair first brought their bags down the path and left Chopper to guard them while they went back for the old man, who was already starting to show signs of waking. They carefully picked him up and brought him to where they'd left their packs before splashing a little bit of water on his face to rouse him.

"Why are we out here?" the old man asked. "Is this part of the game?"

Steve was confused. "What game?"

"The one you were playing with my visitors! Where did they go, anyway?"

"You fell asleep while I was explaining the rules," Clem said, "And your guests had to leave early this morning."

"That was very rude of me!" Ladon said, with tears in his eyes. "How will I ever make it up to them? Will they ever come back?"

"I don't think you need to worry about them," Clem said reassuringly. "They didn't really care much about manners."

This perked the old man up so much that he jumped up and down with excitement, and started singing a song about how everybody loved him, as he skipped down the road. A few minutes later, he stopped and turned around to ask, "Where are we going, anyway?"

"We're going to introduce you to our friend Hazel," Clem replied.

"And her friend Roger." Steve added "You'll like him. You and he have a lot in common."

This news excited Ladon even more. "I'm going to be a guest! I never get to visit people. Should I take a gift?" Before waiting for an answer, he started doing cartwheels and somersaults down the middle of the trail. After a few minutes, the man seemed to get dizzy and plopped down on a rock to rest while Steve and Clem caught up to him.

"So Ladon, what would you do if you met a dragon?" Clem asked.

"I did meet a dragon. Dragons are bad!" Ladon suddenly got nervous, and added whispering, "Never talk to dragons, dragons are evil."

"But what if you met a good dragon?" Steve inquired.

The Dragon Master didn't seem to have understood the good part. "Bad! Bad! Bad! Bad! Bad! Bad! Bad!"

he sang getting up from his rock to run ahead again.

The old man seemed tireless as they walked the long distance. Steve and Clem labored under the weight of their packs. Shortly before they came to the place where they were to meet Ruby, Clem suggested the group stop for a break.

"A picnic!" Ladon said excitedly.

"Yeah, exactly. Let's have a picnic."

They all rested and ate until they felt quite refreshed. Then Clem handed each of them a drink, looking meaningfully at Steve as he did so. Steve understood that Ladon was about to take another nap.

When the old man had fallen asleep yet again, Clem said, "Why don't you and Chopper leave Ladon and me here with the packs, and get Ruby. There's lots of room here for her to land, and we can load up the bags and the old dude. It'll be easier than carrying everything the rest of the way."

"Sounds good," Steve said as he stood up looking at the bulging bags and squaring his shoulders. "I sure hope Hazel can make some use out of all this stuff. I'd hate it if we carried it all this way for nothing."

CHAPTER 12

It was many hours and several rest stops later that Ruby, exhausted by the load, landed just outside their village. Ladon was still asleep, but Clem put an extra drop of sleeping potion in his mouth as a precaution. Then he and Steve left Ruby to rest and Chopper to guard their bags and passenger as they went off to find Hazel.

When they approached the village, they were met with an unexpected and horrible surprise. They could see a thin trail of smoke rising from the place where Roger's house had once stood. Aside from a few stones from the foundation, there was nothing left of the home.

"Whoa, dude!" Clem exclaimed. "What the heck happened there?"

They ran toward the scene and found a few villagers busy clearing rubble and putting out the last of the embers. Steve questioned the first person he met.

"What happened? Are Hazel and Roger alright?"

The old woman had tears in her eyes as she spoke, "It was not long after you left. Two men came and broke into Roger's house. They took Roger and Hazel hostage while they looked for something in the house."

Her husband interrupted her. "At least, that's what we assume happened. No one knew what was going on at first. It was only when my wife went to see Hazel that we realized something was wrong."

The old woman continued, "When no one answered the door, I looked in the window. I saw Roger and Hazel tied up, and two masked men going through their things. I ran to get my husband, but by the time we got back, the house was empty!"

"As we were looking through the house, we heard a noise outside. We ran out to see what it was. Just in time too. A huge dragon set the house on fire."

"A dragon?" Clem and Steve asked together.

"Well," said the man. "We only saw the fireball. The blacksmith was the one who saw the dragon."

"I told Hazel she shouldn't be doing all that dragon research," the old woman said. "Dragons are no good."

"Did the blacksmith get a good look at the dragon? What color did he say it was?" Steve asked.

"I never thought to ask," said the old man. "I didn't know they came in different colors."

"What happened to Hazel and Roger?" Clem asked. "Has anyone seen them? Where are they?"

"No one knows," the old man explained apologetically. "We're guessing that the intruders took them along when they left."

Clem turned to Steve. "We should check out Hazel's place. Maybe they're there."

The villager looked at them in alarm. "Don't leave again! We're having a hard time defending the village against the nightly attacks. Without Roger and Hazel to help, the village will be destroyed!"

Clem turned to the couple and said, "Collect all of the smelliest trash and pile it up at the hardest places to defend. Every day, add more junk to it until there is a wall of garbage around the village. Apparently zombies hate the smell of rotting trash even more than we do. The village won't smell the nicest, but it should make the boundaries much easier to protect."

Steve, remembering the plight of the other village they'd been to, added, "When you're done collecting trash, get some young folks to ride out to nearby villages and tell them the same thing."

The old couple agreed and went off to tell the other villagers of the plan while Clem and Steve ran back to Ruby. She was too tired to take them all to Hazel's in one trip, so they re-secured Ladon and Chopper on the saddle, then Steve climbed on and told her to head to Hazel's house. Clem was left with the heavy bags waiting for the dragon to return.

When Hazel was cursed to live her life as a witch, she lived deep in the woods, in what used to be called the Swamp of Despair. The place was much more cheerful now that the curse had been lifted, but the home was still protected by reputation, spells and a fair number of traps.

As they approached, Steve noticed that none of the traps had been triggered, and her house seemed untouched. He began to feel a sense of optimism, thinking that maybe their friends had escaped here and were safe after all. Once he'd unloaded the Dragon Master and sent Ruby back to Clem, his hopes were dashed. Hazel and Roger were nowhere to be seen.

Steve stashed Ladon in the house and walked the perimeter, making sure no one had tried to break in. He put out food for Chopper and Ruby, and before long, the dragon returned with Clem and all the baggage.

"How are we going to figure out which talisman is the artifact we need to communicate with Ruby? We need Hazel!" Steve asked as he helped Clem unload the saddle.

"What a time to be thinking about that!" Clem scolded him. "Our friends are in danger. We need to rescue them!"

"Oh yeah. Where's my head?" Steve said. "You're right! But where do we start? How do we find out where they've been taken?" His voice was rising as panic welled up inside him.

"Let's take things one step at a time," Clem said calmly. Clem's professional tone calmed Steve down, and together they went inside and sat down at the kitchen table to plan their next move.

"No one saw them leave," Steve said. "So we don't know what direction to start searching in."

"No, but we do have reports of a dragon, so that

might be a clue."

"But if only one person saw it, maybe he was wrong! Maybe it was something else." Steve said.

Clem nodded. "We should be skeptical of everything, but we have to start somewhere."

Steve considered this. "If another dragon is involved, we need to figure out which of this pile of things is the talisman, and how to use it, so we can at least negotiate to get Hazel and Roger back."

"Why don't you start going through the things we got from Ladon's house? Maybe do it outside where Ruby might be able to help," Clem said. "I'll head back to the village and question everyone who might have been a witness to the kidnapping. I'll come back when I'm done, and we can decide what to do based on the information we get over the next few hours."

CHAPTER 13

After Clem had dosed the Dragon Master with some more sleeping potion and headed off toward the village, Steve got to work. He gathered up a pile of things they had taken along from the old man's home and brought them outside, where he carefully laid them out. He called Ruby over, and she settled down in the grass nearby. Chopper cuddled against the curve of her tail, and promptly fell asleep.

Steve began working his way through the artifacts. One by one he held, rubbed and wore the items and spoke to the dragon to see if there was any change. One by one, his attempts failed, and the items were thrown onto the growing pile of junk on the hill behind him.

Hours later, Ruby fell asleep, and Steve was feeling disheartened about the chances of finding anything that would work. He barely looked at the amulet that was next up when he put it around his neck.

Suddenly, he was flying through the air. His wings

flapped gracefully, and he felt happy and exhilarated at the wonder of flight and the beauty of the landscape around him. He felt the wind beneath his wings and the cold air as it entered his nostrils. Around him, he saw dozens of dragons, beautiful dragons, flying together as a family. His family.

Then his brain began to realize he wasn't a dragon. He was Steve. He couldn't fly. His heart stopped for a moment as he panicked. He anticipated a fall of many hundreds of meters. As he opened his mouth to scream, his brain once again kicked in to remind him that this could not be real. It had to be a dream.

Steve breathed a sigh of relief and told himself to wake up. When he realized he was awake, panic rose again. None of this was making any sense. Unless... could this be Ruby's dream?

Steve grasped at the amulet around his neck and pulled it off. As soon as he released the gem, his world came back into focus. He lay back on the grass, breathing deeply, glad to be back in reality, and pleased that he seemed to have found the artifact he'd been looking for.

After he pulled himself together, he got up and gave Ruby a nudge. "Wake up, I think I've found something!"

The dragon reluctantly opened one eye and gazed at Steve with irritation, as if he had awakened her from a pleasant dream.

"Sorry, Ruby. I know it was a great dream, I saw it."

She tilted her head and looked at him inquisitively. Steve took a deep breath and put the amulet back on. This time, he closed his eyes and tried to focus his mind on what he had seen in the dream just moments before. He tried his best to project this image toward Ruby.

He wasn't sure at first if he was succeeding. Then suddenly he somehow felt the dragon sharing the image, sharpening parts of it and fading others until their focus was on two dragons flying together not far in the distance. Steve felt a surge of affection and love towards the pair.

"Are those your parents?" Steve asked Ruby.

Suddenly, the image in his mind changed, and he saw a very young red dragon hatchling being lovingly nuzzled by her parents. "Wow," Steve said in awe.

This happy vision was interrupted suddenly by a shrill scream. Steve opened his eyes and saw Ladon running out of the house and toward Ruby waving his cane menacingly. The old man was screaming, "Bad dragon! Die dragon! Bad! Bad! Bad!"

Steve stood up quickly and moved to tackle the Dragon Master before he reached Ruby. Once Steve had him immobilized on the ground, he tried to calm the old man down. "Ladon, calm down. This is Ruby. She's a friend. Not a bad dragon. A good one."

Ladon was hearing none it. He continued his chant of, "Bad, bad, bad, bad."

Steve, forgetting about the amulet, called out to Ruby, "Get out of sight for a few minutes so I can calm him down."

Ruby must have sensed his meaning, because she

and Chopper moved off into the woods nearby. When they were out of sight, Steve shook Ladon and said in a loud voice, "Wake up! You were having a nightmare."

"I was?" the old man asked.

"Yeah, you were screaming something about a dragon. But as you can see, there are no dragons here!"

Ladon looked around. "Oh yeah."

Steve got up off of the old man and helped him up. "Are you feeling better now?"

"Better than what?"

"Um, never mind," Steve said. "Let's go in and find something to eat."

As the Dragon Master followed him into the house, Steve received a mental image from Ruby. It was an image of the old man. Steve was confused, and then the picture in his mind focused on the amulet around Ladon's neck. Steve sighed and mumbled under his breath, "Great, Ruby. How am I supposed to convince him to do that?"

Chapter 14

Steve and Ladon were in the kitchen snacking on some apples when Clem returned.

"Hey Steve, I didn't realize you were still here. I didn't see Ruby, and you left a large pile of trash outside. Didn't you have any luck?"

"More luck than you could ever imagine," Steve answered, subtly gesturing towards the Dragon Master.

Ladon perked up. "Where is Ruby? Who is Ruby? Will Ruby be my friend?"

"Ruby would love to be your friend, dude," Clem said. "But first I think it's time for a nap."

"Really?" Ladon asked. "I sure have been sleeping a lot; I must be tired."

"Yep, it's definitely your bedtime. Look, it's almost dark." Clem got up and said, "How about I get you a cup of warm milk to settle you down?"

Once Ladon was happily snoring in his cot, Steve began filling Clem in on how he'd found the amulet and how it worked. "It's not what I expected," Steve said. "The way dragons speak isn't actually a language, it's more like mind-reading."

"You've got to let me try that thing!" Clem said.

"You'll get your chance," Steve replied. "But Ruby said she wanted me to put it on Ladon."

"Seriously, dude?"

Steve shrugged, "Maybe she thinks she can talk crazy as well as you can. Anyway, we may as well try it now. I can't see us being able to get it on him when he's awake. At least not without hurting him. He's terrified of all things dragon."

Steve tried his best to send a message to Ruby that he was going to put the amulet on the old man. Then he slipped it off his head and gently placed it around the sleeping man's neck.

Almost immediately, Ladon started tossing and turning in his sleep. Clem looked at Steve, "Now what?" he asked.

"I guess we'll just leave it on until he wakes up. Ruby can stop communicating whenever she wants, so let's just trust her to do whatever she needs to."

Clem shrugged in agreement as they left the old man to his fitful sleep and went back to the table.

"So what did you find out about Hazel and Roger?" Steve asked.

"I've pieced together a few things," Clem replied. "First, the kidnappers had help from inside the village. The timing was just too perfect for it to be a coincidence. Second, the kidnappers left the village from the West gate, and all eyewitnesses saw them follow the road in the same direction."

"What about the dragon that supposedly was with them?"

"I only found one person who claimed to have actually seen a dragon. He seemed trustworthy, but with only one eyewitness, I'm not putting a lot of faith in the account."

"What's our next move?" Steve asked.

"Let's gather some supplies. I'm sure Hazel has some good potions around here that could help us."

"What about Ladon?"

"We'll find him a babysitter before we go," Clem said.

"Who do you hate that much?"

"We'll just have to pay enough to make it worth their suffering."

When Ladon woke up, it was immediately clear that a babysitter might not be needed. The old man walked to the table and surprised Clem and Steve by calmly peering over their shoulders. "Hey guys, thanks for putting up with me all night. What are you up to?"

Steve's jaw nearly hit the floor. Clem recovered his wits first and replied "I'm glad you're feeling better, dude."

"I'm a little fuzzy on what's real and what's not. Was I really as crazy as I think I was?"

"Um, if you think you were completely and violently insane, then yeah, that sounds about right."

"And did I hit you with my cane?"

"I could show you the bruises," Steve said.

Ladon looked dismayed. "I'm really sorry, guys." He paused for a moment before asking, "And the red dragon? That was just my imagination, right?"

Clem looked the old man up and down trying to detect signs of any remaining insanity, then said, "Don't freak out on us, but the dragon is real. I think she's the one who cured your crazy."

"You're not kidding?" Ladon said, still not fully believing Clem. "There really is a red dragon?"

Steve was the one who replied. "You've still got the amulet around your neck. Why don't you ask her? We call her Ruby, and she's nearby."

Ladon looked down at his chest where the amulet was resting. "I never noticed. I thought I'd thrown this out, or lost it. Did you know I went to talk to the Ender dragon?"

"Yeah," Clem replied. "We think that's what made you crazy in the first place. I'm guessing that dragon was pretty angry?"

"Completely deranged. And having him in my head... well, it wasn't good for my health, I guess."

"Ruby's not at all like that," Steve said. "She's not angry. She's amazing. I hope you get a chance to talk to her later, but right now we need some information."

"I'll do what I can," Ladon replied. "What's going on and how can I help?"

It was Clem who answered, "Our friends have been kidnapped. One witness said that there was a dragon at the scene. Do you think the Ender dragon could be involved? You're the only one who's been in his head. What can you tell us that could help us find and defeat him?"

Chapter 15

The next morning Clem and Steve said farewell to Ladon, leaving him in the safety of Hazel's cabin. The Dragon Master had been a wealth of information about the Ender Dragon and had given Steve tips on how to use the amulet to talk to Ruby. Promising to return as soon as possible, Steve, Clem, Chopper, and Ruby flew off in pursuit of the kidnappers.

After hours of flying, Steve was beginning to lose hope. He called out to Clem, "Maybe they went in a different direction after they were out of sight. Maybe they only took that road as a diversion."

"It's the only lead we have," Clem replied. "Don't give up yet."

"Let's land and scout around for a bit," Steve said. "Maybe Chopper can pick up their scent."

"Good idea," replied Clem. "Beam Ruby a landing signal."

Once they landed on the ground, it didn't take long

for Chopper to find a scent. He led them forward at a steady pace until they reached a large clearing, where they stopped and gaped at the sight before them.

It was a massive army of skeletons. Steve had never seen so many in one place. They weren't attacking; they were just standing there at the other end of the field.

Steve grabbed Chopper and put him on Ruby's back, projecting a command for her to fly to safety. She quickly lifted off and the skeletons made no move to try and stop her. Steve and Clem both stared at the motionless monsters. "Is it just me, or do you find this a little weird too?" Steve asked.

"Not just you, dude" Clem replied, not taking his eyes off the monsters, "This isn't usual skeleton behavior." A movement from the middle of the monster army caught his attention. "Something's happening."

As they watched, a skeleton carrying a white banner came walking toward the front of the crowd. It didn't stop as he reached the front. It continued on and did not pause until it had reached the halfway point between the skeleton army and Steve and Clem.

"Have you ever known a skeleton to wave a white flag?" Steve asked Clem.

"Nope. And if you'd asked me before this very moment, I would have said they didn't know what a white flag meant. They're not big on peace. Or surrender."

"I didn't think so," Steve said. "So, what do we do now?"

"Well, I guess we should go up there and see what happens."

Steve thought for a moment then said, "Yeah, but maybe I should go alone. At least one of us should survive if this is a trap, and with the diamond chest-plate and enchanted sword, I might have a better chance of getting out of there unhurt if it turns out to be a trap."

"But I'm the more experienced fighter!" Clem protested.

"That's why you need to stay alive!" Steve said. "If I die, you need to save Hazel and Roger."

Clem looked hurt, but slowly nodded in agreement. "Okay, but be careful. Come back safe."

"That's the plan," Steve said as he dropped his pack by Clem, gripped his sword tightly and walked forward to meet the waiting skeleton.

He stopped a few feet in front of the creature anticipating an attack. He was surprised when the skeleton held out a sheet of paper toward him. He didn't reach for it right away, but the skeleton remained motionless, holding out the note.

Not seeing any further danger, Steve took a step forward, snatched the paper from the skeleton's outstretched hand, then immediately retreated.

Having delivered its message, the skeleton turned around and walked back into the crowd of monsters. Steve watched it go, then turned and dashed back to where Clem was waiting.

Together they looked at the message. It read, "If you ever what to see your friends alive again, bring the sword and chest-plate to the End Portal at the edge of the Snowy Mountains of Agondray"

Clem looked up. "No," he said.

Steve was flabbergasted. "What?!" he yelled at Clem. "You don't want to save Roger and Hazel?"

"We're not giving anybody anything until we know that they aren't already dead," Clem told him. "There's a quill in my pack, see if you can dig it up."

While Steve rummaged through the pack, Clem looked over their map to find the nearest village.

When Steve handed him the quill, Clem flipped over the skeleton's note and began writing on the back: "There is a village two miles west of here. We'll be staying at the inn. Deliver a note from our friends to us there. We will bring you the chest plate and sword only when we know that Hazel and Roger are safe, not before."

Clem tied the note to an arrow, and shot it high up into the air. It landed right in the middle of the field where Steve had met the skeleton earlier. Clem grabbed his pack, and said to Steve, "Now we wait." Then he turned around and started walking down the path they had come.

Steve waited a few moments to make sure the skeleton army wouldn't pursue. He sent a telepathic message to Ruby to follow the skeletons at a distance to see where they delivered the message, then he shouldered his pack and followed Clem.

Chapter 16

When they arrived at the inn, Steve and Clem brought out their map and Steve pointed out some of the landmarks that Ruby had sent Steve telepathically.

"They're obviously heading to Agondray," Steve said.

"That's great. If we attempt a rescue, it'll look like we're following their directions to meet up there for a trade, " Clem said. "But at their current pace they won't get there for a while, so we should get some rest. Neither of us has gotten very much sleep lately."

"Probably a good idea, but I don't know if I can sleep. I'm too worried about Hazel and Roger," Steve replied. "Well, mostly Hazel."

"Need some sleeping potion? I still have some left."

"Nope," Steve shook his head adamantly. "Don't you dare drug me, Clem."

"Wouldn't dream of it, dude," Clem said with a smile as he headed toward one of the beds in the room.

The night was approaching, and both men were fast asleep when Chopper came bounding into the room. The dog pounced on Steve and began licking his face mercilessly.

"Hey, Chopper. I guess you and Ruby got back okay." Steve sent a non-verbal greeting to Ruby as well.

Steve noticed that Clem hadn't woken up. "Hey Clem, wake up! Ruby and Chopper are back."

When Clem still didn't wake up, Chopper decided it would be a good idea to say hello to him anyway.

"Oof!" Clem exclaimed as Chopper landed heavily on the mercenary's stomach.

Steve barely noticed Clem's commotion as Ruby had started sending him information on the location of the skeleton's hideout. He lit a few torches to brighten the room and started a fire in the fireplace. He then grabbed the map and started searching the area of the mountain range for clues. "I wish this map had more detail," he told Clem. "According to Ruby, the skeletons entered a cave system in one of these mountains. It's got a pretty distinctive peak, so I think I can find it when we get there, but it's not obvious on the map."

"I hope that's where Roger and Hazel are being held," Clem replied. "I'm hoping Hazel will sneak some helpful information in the note she writes for us."

Steve looked at Clem with admiration. "Whoa! She could do that, couldn't she? I thought you just asked for the note so Ruby could find out where they went!"

Clem smiled back at Steve. "You're learning, kid. Why don't you ask Ruby about the entrance to the caves, and whether she saw more than one?"

Steve concentrated and tried to form those questions into images. He was surprised at how well Ruby understood his horrible attempts at communicating. "She says she saw two entrances that were definitely part of the same cave system. She saw skeletons at both. There were lots of other cave openings, but they may not lead anywhere."

Steve paused as he gathered more information. "The main entrance isn't far up the mountain. That's where the skeletons went in and out. The other entrance was high up on a cliff face. She only saw one skeleton inside that part of the cave."

"Okay, so that's our entrance," Clem said. "If Hazel tells us we need to do a rescue rather than a trade, we'll go in there. Even if we go ahead with the trade, it's going to happen over here," he pointed to a spot on the map. "Maybe one of us should fly with Ruby up near that top cave and make sure we're not double-crossed."

"But they'll notice a red dragon flying around the mountain!"

"That's why we have to get Ruby to fly to the top, where she won't be seen. Hopefully the terrain will allow for a safe climb down to the cave."

"Okay," Steve said, "I guess that makes sense, but it's a pretty sketchy plan."

"We'll know more when we get the note from Hazel," Clem explained. "Until then, sketchy is the best we can do."

Steve ordered for some food to come up to their

room while Clem packed their bags with the supplies they'd need for a rescue. They were so intent on the task, they were startled when there was a knock on the door.

"It's probably our dinner," Clem said.

Steve opened the door to find a frightened-looking innkeeper standing there with a platter of food in one hand and an arrow in the other.

The man handed the arrow to Steve. "This was, um, delivered to the town gate this evening." The man's voice quaked just a bit. "I think it's for you."

Steve looked at the arrow. A note was attached. "Ah, yeah. I think we've been expecting this."

"And your food," said the innkeeper, holding out the platter.

"Thanks, dude," Clem said from behind Steve as he reached for their dinner and handed the man several coins in exchange.

"Is there anything else you need?" The innkeeper looked hesitantly at Clem.

"Don't worry," the mercenary replied. "We'll be leaving at first light."

Steve recognized a look of relief in the man's face as he retreated back down the hallway.

CHAPTER 17

Steve ignored the food as he examined the arrow. The note was wrapped around the shaft, with bold, messy letters declaring it was to be delivered to the strangers at the inn immediately. Untying the knotted twine holding the letter in place, he unrolled the paper and brought it to the table where Clem had already started in on the food.

The note was clearly in Hazel's neat printing, but to Steve it made very little sense. "It sounds like she wants us to deliver the armor and do the trade," Steve said. "I guess the rescue plans are off."

"Don't be so hasty. Let's take a closer look at this thing," Clem mused.

"It's weirdly worded, but the note seems pretty clear," Steve said. "What are we looking for?"

"Does this sound anything like Hazel? Even a little bit, dude?"

"Well, no..."

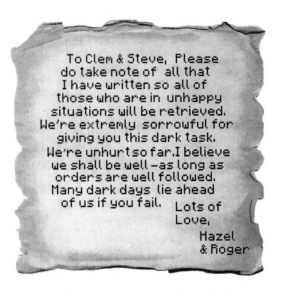

To Clem & Steve, Please
do take note of all that
I have written so all of
those who are in unhappy
situations will be retrieved.
We're extremly sorrowful for
giving you this dark task.
We're unhurt so far. I believe
we shall be well – as long as
orders are well followed.
Many dark days lie ahead
of us if you fail. Lots of
Love,

Hazel
& Roger

"So, let's assume that she wrote it this way for a reason," Clem explained. "She had to make it sound like she was convincing us to go along so her captors wouldn't suspect anything, but there must be a hidden meaning for us in here somewhere."

Steve got excited. "Like a code?" He asked. "Maybe it's the first letter of every word." He looked at the note again, then shook his head. "Every second word?"

"Nope and nope," said Clem.

"Maybe the last letter of every word?"

"Nope."

"All the capitalized letters?"

"Nope."

"Read it backwards?"

"Nope."

"Does anything pop out when you look at it upside down?"

"Nope."

"How about invisible ink?"

Clem heated the paper slightly near the fire. "Nope again."

"Well," Steve said in exasperation. "Do you have any idea of how to read the secret message?"

"Nope."

Steve grabbed some food and collapsed into a chair. "Well, that's helpful."

Clem continued to stare at the note. "Maybe we're looking at this wrong."

"What do you mean?"

"I mean, we're looking at the words," Clem mused.

Steve, feeling frustrated, spat out, "What else would we look at. The tears in the paper?"

Clem looked at him impressed. "Now that's thinking outside the box," he said. "Good job, dude!"

"Really? There might be some message in the tears in the paper?"

"Well, no," Clem said as he examined the edges of the page. "But at least you're looking at it creatively now."

Steve came back to the table and stared at the parchment again. "Did you notice that the lines all start in different places? At first I thought it was centered, but really, it's just random."

Clem took another look. "Yeah, you're right. And look, she misspelled 'extremely.' She wouldn't usually make a mistake like that."

Steve was getting excited. "Maybe she did both those

things so she could line up certain letters vertically in the note?"

Clem gave Steve a whack on the back. "I think you might be right." He ran his finger down the page. "Most of these don't line up, but here... look at this!"

Under the letter C that started Clem's name, there seemed to be a straight line of letters. "C-A-V-E-I-X-G-U-A-R-D-S, Steve read out as Clem wrote down the letters.

To Clem & Steve, Please
do take note of all that
I have written so all of
those who are in unhappy
situations will be retrieved.
We're extremly sorrowful for
giving you this dark task.
We're unhurt so far. I believe
we shall be well —as long as
orders are well followed.
Many dark days lie ahead
of us if you fail. Lots of
Love,

Hazel
& Roger

"They're in a cave, and there are guards," Clem muttered. "The IX must be the Roman numeral nine. That's too bad. That's an awful lot of guards to deal with. We might have to do the trade after all."

"Look here," Steve said. "There's another bunch of letters that are lined up!" He pointed to the page under the capital letter P in the first line.

"P-L-A-N-T-O-K-I-L-L-A-L-L," Clem said as he wrote down the letters. "Plan to kill all? Well, I guess we're back to rescue. It sounds like they plan to kill Hazel and Roger, and us too, once they get what they want."

Steve grunted and returned to his chair, slouching as he chewed some bread.

"What's the problem?" Clem asked him. "I thought you wanted to go ahead with the rescue?"

"Why didn't Hazel use my name in the code? Doesn't she think I'm important?" As soon as the words left his lips, Steve's face flushed in embarrassment.

"Dude!" Clem exclaimed. "Are you kidding me?"

Steve sighed. "Sorry. I know it's ridiculous. I just felt a little jealous since she used your name in the secret code and not mine. I'm over it now."

"I should hope so!" Clem shook his head. "So, are we ready to launch a rescue?"

"Ready as we're ever going to be," Steve replied. "The sun's coming up. Let's get moving."

CHAPTER 18

After some debate, Steve and Clem decided to fly directly to the Mountains of Agondray. If it made the skeletons suspicious, that was a risk they would have to take. As a precaution, they asked Ruby to keep them out of sight by flying through clouds and over heavy forests.

Steve was the first one to catch a glimpse of the mountain peak where the enemy was hiding out. "There," he pointed out a landmark to Clem as they flew by. "That one that looks like it's got a bite out of the peak. That's the mountain."

"I see it," Clem called back. "I see the lower cave entrance too, but where's the upper entrance."

Steve squinted out at the mountain. "See the shadow about two-thirds of the way up? Look at the left of that."

Clem stared for a moment before he saw it too. "Ok, let's stop over there. It's close enough that an arrow can reach the caves, but there's enough cover for us to hide. Even Ruby."

Steve sent the landing location to Ruby, and in a few minutes they were looking out through some large boulders at the lower entrance. There was a lot of activity there, with at least a few skeletons standing in the cave's dark shadows at all times. At the upper entrance, they saw only one skeleton standing guard.

"The guards seem to be mostly concentrated on the lower level. I think that's where they think an attack is most likely," Clem said.

"So we should attack the top?"

"No, we should attack both at once," Clem said. "If we both go up, the guards below will just run up, and then we'll both be up there with no easy means of escape."

"So, what's the plan?" Steve asked the more experienced man.

"You get on Ruby. I'm going to take out the single guard up top with an arrow, then start firing like crazy into the lower cave to see how many I can pick off. Once they start coming out, I'll show myself and attack." Clem scratched his head. "If there's nine of them like Hazel said, I'll see if I can take care of at least three or four of them before I run in. The rest shouldn't be too hard. It'll be like a slow night back at the village."

Steve grinned. "Do you think Hazel and Roger are up at the top or the bottom?"

"If it were me, I'd keep them at the top," Clem said, "But by splitting up, we've got the best chance of finding them quickly."

"So, if one of us finds them, what then?" Steve asked.

"Get them out as quickly as possible," Clem said. "Then play it by ear. If I think you're in trouble, or if you think I am, come to the rescue." Clem grinned at him. "That's what you'd do anyway, isn't it?"

Steve grinned, "You know it."

Clem laughed and pounded Steve on the back.

Steve suddenly remembered another potential issue. "There's probably a group waiting to ambush us at the meeting place," Steve reminded Clem. "When we don't show, they'll know that we're mounting a rescue. How far away are they from here?"

Clem glanced at the map. "It would take them about 20 minutes walking to get here, I think. Maybe more, since they have to stay in the shadow of the mountain. It should be enough time for us to get in and out." Then he began sorting through his pack for things they might need. He handed Steve a bow and some arrows. "I'm not sure what you're going to face up there," he said. "Just because there's only one guard we can see, it doesn't mean there aren't more of them deeper in the cavern."

"I'll keep my eyes open," Steve said confidently, aware that most of his confidence came from his enchanted diamond chest plate. "You take care of yourself too. You're taking on far more than I am." He thought a moment before adding, "Take Chopper with you. He's a good fighter, and he'll probably be more useful to you than he will to me."

Clem scratched the dog behind his ears and said,

"I'll be glad to have him with me." Chopper wagged his tail in reply.

Steve relayed the plan to Ruby, hopped on her back, and within moments they had taken off and headed for the cover of the clouds.

CHAPTER 19

After leaving Clem at his vantage point, Ruby flew up over the top of the mountain with Steve. They stayed out of site of the skeletons in the cave below until they saw the first volley of arrows that Clem sent toward the skeletons guarding the entrances. He first took out one at the upper cave entrance, then quickly focused all his arrows on the lower, main cave. If all went according to plan, the enemy would focus their defense there, and Steve would be able to sneak into the upper cave without attracting too much attention.

Steve counted to ten slowly, giving the skeleton guards time to run to defend their main entrance, and for Clem and Chopper to mount their main attack, then he and Ruby flew straight for the cave. Once they were close enough to the entrance, he jumped in and allowed Ruby to fly back out of sight.

The cave was empty. Apparently the single guard that Clem took out with his arrow had been the only defender. Steve looked around for pathways to the rest of the cave system. He saw two possible tunnels to follow. He listened carefully at the first. The sounds of battle were strong there. It must lead to the lower cave. He went to the second cave, wandered a few feet in, and called out with as much volume as he dared, "Hazel. Roger. Are you here?"

He did not receive an answer from his friends. Instead, two skeletons appeared from a cave further down the tunnel and charged at Steve. Realizing that the tunnel he was in would make it difficult to use his sword, he retreated quickly to the larger cave. The two skeletons, key-holed in the tunnel, had no choice but to attack him one at a time. Steve made short work of the first one. The second retreated, and pulled out a bow and arrow.

The first arrow glanced off Steve's armor harmlessly, but it was clear he couldn't just stand there and hope that the next arrows wouldn't strike him in the head. He'd have to go in after the creature and attack it. The skeleton was pulling out another arrow when Steve attacked. He sprinted full-speed, with his sword in front of him like a lance. The skeleton, startled by Steve's approach, never got off a shot. It was impaled on Steve's enchanted sword before it had regained its wits.

Steve ran toward the place where the skeletons had first appeared, figuring the only reason they'd be hanging around was to guard something. He just hoped that something was Hazel and Roger.

Turning the corner, he saw them both, tied up in the

corner of the room with their backs to him. "Hazel! Are you OK?" he called out. "Roger?" The only response he got was a sharp jerk of Hazel's head, directing him to look downward.

"Oh man. This is bad!" Steve muttered as he saw what she had been trying to tell him. The floor was covered in pressure plates. He wasn't sure what would happen if he stepped on one, but he doubted it would be good. "There must be a path! Hazel, how did they get you in there?"

Hazel's head jerked again. This time up to the ceiling. There was some sort of mechanism up there. Steve guessed that it had been used to drop his friends down past the traps. Whatever it had been, it looked irreparably damaged now. There was no way he could use it. Neither could the skeletons, which was more proof that they'd never intended to let Hazel and Roger go.

Steve gazed around the room, looking for some other way to reach the corner without triggering the pressure plates. Abandoning thoughts of using the contraption on the ceiling, he noticed white bars sticking out of the walls at regular intervals. He walked to the nearest one and examined it more closely. It wasn't a torch, but it was giving off an eerie light. He reached out and tentatively touched it. Nothing happened. He reached out again and grabbed it with his whole hand this time, testing its strength. It might hold his weight, he thought. He lifted his feet from the floor, an idea hatching in his brain. The bar creaked a little, but remained solid.

Stretching out, he reached for the next rod and grasped it firmly. "This could work," he said as he began swinging his body to increase momentum. With one push, he released his back hand and swung forward to grasp the next rod. His fingertips grazed it, but he couldn't find a grip. Dangling from one arm, he decided to use both hands to hold tight to the rod he was hanging from. He began building momentum again, then threw his right hand toward the next rod. This time he caught it solidly.

Having learned from his past error, he brought his left hand up to grasp the same rod, then continued to swing forward, from one bar to the next. He was feeling confident for the next few minutes as he swung from bar to bar. It was then that his hands started to burn. It started as a mild pain in the palms of his hands, but within a few more bars became a nearly unbearable burning sensation. With nowhere to land but a pressure plate if he were to let go, he took a deep breath to try to block out the pain, and resolved to continue.

His vision was fogged with sweat and tears when he finally got to the corner of the room where Hazel and Roger were bound and gagged. The only place for him to land was on the chairs currently occupied by his friends. Reaching out one foot, he attempted to reach the edge of Hazel's chair. She saw what he was attempting and tried to make a little room on her seat.

Steve's toe just barely reached the edge of the chair. Roger, finally understanding what Steve was attempting to do, squeezed a little room on the edge of his chair as well. Steve moved his hands to the very end of the bar he was holding to give himself a better angle, positioned both feet, then pushed himself off the wall and onto the chairs. He flailed a moment before leaning forward and awkwardly grabbing on to Hazel and Roger to balance himself.

A moment later, he pulled the gag out of Hazel's mouth. "Fancy meeting you here," he said, as he rubbed his hands to try and ease the lingering pain.

Chapter 20

Hazel licked her dry lips, then grinned at him. "Steve! I'm so glad to see you! I was worried you wouldn't be able to decipher my note!"

Steve was busy working on the knots holding Hazel to her chair. "Thanks for the heads-up about the guards. Clem knocked out at least two before we came in. I got two in the hallway, and Clem is hopefully dealing with the remaining five down in the lower cavern. We should hurry, though. He might need help."

When Hazel was untied, she quickly helped remove the ropes holding Roger. "So, how do we get out of here?" she asked, looking around. "I don't think I'd be able to swing around the room like you just did."

"I'm not so sure I could do it again, either," Steve admitted. "I don't suppose you have any magic tricks that could fly us to the other end of the room?"

"If only I'd known that I was going to be kidnapped and held in a booby-trapped room, only to be rescued by someone without a plan," Hazel muttered sarcastically. "I would've packed something before I left the house."

Roger, who had finally gotten the gag out of his mouth, chimed in. "Hey, guys. Don't argue. We aren't totally without resources here!"

"What do you mean, Roger?" Steve asked.

"Well, we've got two chairs, a fair amount of rope, your enchanted sword and chest plate, Hazel's brains, and my shrewd business sense."

Hazel turned on her friend and asked, "And how is that shrewd business sense of yours going to help us now, Roger?"

Roger barely missed a beat. "Would you like to buy a chair, Steve?"

Steve wasn't listening, however. "Hazel, what was that contraption that dropped you down here?"

"It was some sort of upside-down track, I think," she replied.

"Roger, help me give Hazel a boost up. If we both stand on chairs and lift Hazel as high as we can, maybe she can get a better look at it."

Steve and Hazel maneuvered themselves so each of them stood on a chair while Hazel squirmed in between them carefully so as not to touch any of the surrounding pressure plates. They tried to lift her but only succeeded in nearly losing their balance.

"OK. Let's try something else," Steve said. "Roger, hold still and hold your body as stiff as your can. Hazel, try to climb up on us. If you can get on one or both of our shoulders, you should be able to reach."

After a few minutes of struggle, Hazel was balanced on Steve's shoulders. "Good job, Hazel. We know it can hold your weight. Is there enough room between the track and the ceiling to hold on to?"

"I think so, yes," she said as she felt along the beam. "More room than I thought there would be."

"Do you think you could get across the room that way?"

Hazel considered for only a second before replying, "Definitely. But once I'm across, how are you going to get up here?"

Steve handed her the rope that had been used to tie Roger to his chair. "Before you cross, tie this to the beam. Roger and I can climb the rope to get up."

She did as Steve instructed, and before long, she had shuffled her way across the beam to land on the other side of the room. Roger followed at a much slower pace and Steve impatiently waited for him. "Hurry up, Roger. We need to get out of here," he called out.

"I don't want to get a splinter," Roger whined.

"Well, I don't want to get dead!"

Roger increased his pace and shortly all three were heading out the door. "Where's Clem?" Hazel asked Steve.

Steve took them to the end of the corridor and pointed down the second shaft. "When I came in, all the sounds of fighting were coming from there."

They listened for a moment. "Well, I don't hear anything now," Hazel said. "Should we go down?"

Steve called out to Ruby with his mind, asking about Clem. She hadn't seen him, and that worried Steve. "I'm going to go down and see if Clem's okay. You two stand by the entrance. Ruby's on her way. She'll take you to safety."

"Ruby?" Hazel gasped. "You've learned how to speak to Ruby?"

"Long story, and it involves a house guest at your cabin, but I'll fill you in later," Steve said. "Go now. I'm going to find Clem."

Steve ran down the corridor, checking over his shoulder to make sure Hazel and Roger were heading toward the mouth of the cave. He breathed a sigh of relief when Ruby let him know they had been picked up and were heading to safety. Now, his only concern was Clem and Chopper. What could be keeping them?

CHAPTER 21

He followed the sounds of battle down the passage-ways, until he saw a bright light up ahead. Slowing down and proceeding cautiously, he crept forward as silently as possible toward the battle that was raging on ahead of him. When he reached the entrance to the large cavern he stopped, pressing himself against the wall to stay out of sight. What he saw made him cringe.

Clem was backed against a wall and surrounded by more than a dozen skeletons and zombies. While he was fighting valiantly, Steve saw that he was tiring. Scanning the room for Chopper, he saw his dog curled up in pain in the shadows of the cave. Steve decided a dramatic entrance might give Clem a chance to get the upper hand. He ran into the room waving his sword and yelling at the top of his lungs.

His plan worked. A good number of the monsters turned their attention to him. He began slashing at them wildly, wondering if maybe his plan had been too effective.

Clem shouted a greeting over the noise of battle, "Nice entrance, dude!"

Steve sliced through two skeleton warriors at once as he replied, "Thanks. It looked like you could use some help."

"Are Hazel and Roger alive?" the mercenary inquired.

"Yeah. They're with Ruby, safe and sound."

"That's good," Clem shouted. "I'd hate for anything to happen to Hazel before I get a chance to kill her."

"What?" called out Steve, thinking he must have heard wrong. "You want to kill Hazel?"

"Look around. Does this look like nine guards?"

Steve grimaced as he pulled his sword out of a zombie's chest. "I see your point," he yelled back. The crowd of monsters was starting to thin out as the pair continued their attack. "What happened to Chopper? Is he alright?"

"He's hurt, but a bit of healing potion will fix him up just fine," Clem replied. "Now that you're here, we should be out of this cave in a few minutes."

When there were only two skeletons left standing Steve ran toward Chopper, leaving Clem to finish the battle. When he reached his dog, he cradled his best friend in his arms and said gently, "Hey Chopper, did you miss me?"

Chopper weakly wagged his tail and gave Steve a small lick, then whimpered.

"We'll get you to safety, boy. Then Hazel will fix

you right up." Steve whispered with tears in his eyes.

"Let's get out of here," Clem called out from where he had eliminated the last of the skeletons. "I want to get out of these caves," he said. "Blue sky is sounding just about perfect right now."

Steve gathered Chopper in his arms and followed Clem toward the exit. The mercenary had nearly reached the blue sky he was craving when Steve heard a loud rumble.

"Hurry," Clem called out. "I think the tunnel is unstable."

The words had barely reached Steve's ears before a large chunk of the tunnel tumbled down right in front of him. He called out to his friend in concern, "Clem! Are you okay?"

"Yeah," Clem replied. "But you're stuck!"

Steve put Chopper down and began trying to clear some of the rubble, and Clem did the same from the other side of the cave-in, but more dirt and stone kept falling to remove whatever progress they made. After a few minutes, Clem's face appeared in a small hole near the top right-hand side of the cave.

"There's a little hole here," he said. "Maybe we can make it bigger."

Steve shook his head. "I'm going to pass Chopper through to you. Get him out of here. I already asked Ruby for a pick-up. She should be out there soon if she's not already waiting. I'm going to go back to the top entrance and have her pick me up from there."

Once Clem had the wounded dog, Steve doubled

back and headed back to the upper chambers. The cave-in had caused some rubble to build up in his path, but he was grateful there was nothing large enough to keep him from following his original trail. He was even more grateful that there were no more monsters in sight at all. As he passed the room where Roger and Hazel had been kept, he spied the cave entrance and breathed a sigh of relief. The rescue had been a success, and there was nothing left to do but fly his friends home.

He opened his mind to Ruby, both to check on his companions and to let her know that he was ready to be picked up. What he saw turned his relief into dread. His mind's eye saw that his friends were cowering behind a rock while Ruby's eyes were focused on the one thing he had never expected to see: the Ender Dragon.

CHAPTER 22

Seeing the scene through Ruby's eyes, he watched in horror as the black dragon swooped forward, heading straight for his friends. Ruby flew directly into the Ender Dragon's path, and Steve closed his eyes for a moment, shutting his mind to the battle as the two giant beasts ascended quickly into the sky.

Steve tried to recover from the dizziness that overcame him by pulling off the amulet and staring out of the cave for a moment. Before he could tune back into the battle, he saw something out of the corner of his eye that made him forget the dragons for the moment. A large group of soldiers was heading toward the caves. In the shadows, Steve could see skeletons in their midst as well.

"This isn't good," he muttered to himself. They must be the group that was sent to the meeting place where they were expecting delivery of the chest-plate and sword. It wouldn't be long now before they reached the mouth of the cave, and then it would only be a matter of time before they found him. He had to get out of there fast.

Steve blocked out all thoughts of the dragons locked in combat in the skies above and looked at the rocks that surrounded him. There was a small ledge right before the cave entrance, and he could see a series of rocks and cracks he could use to climb. It would be dangerous, but staying in the cave was not an option he could afford to consider and, given the battle that was raging on the top of the mountain, he was going to have to do it on his own.

Taking a deep breath, Steve stepped off the ledge and jammed his fingers into the first crevice in the rock above him. He found a small rock he could wedge his foot onto, and pushed himself up. Steadily and carefully, he continued upward until his chest burned with every breath, and his fingers ached from supporting his weight.

Steve felt for his next foothold on the rocky cliff. He really didn't want to look down. He wasn't sure how high he was, but he knew if he slipped and fell, death would certainly await him. His muscles ached from the strain of climbing. Looking up he saw that he was still a long way from the top. He was beginning to worry he wouldn't make it.

His foot found a hold, and he pushed himself up enough to grasp at a crag in the cliff-face with his hand. Painfully, he pulled himself a few inches higher.

He found another foothold and put his weight on

it. He felt the ground slip beneath him. He grasped at the cliff with his free hand but found nothing but loose dirt and air. Dangling by only one hand, Steve forced himself not to panic. He searched with his feet for a foothold, and quickly found one that would support his weight.

Relief flooded through him. Looking around for his next handhold, he saw something from his new position. It looked like a small cave in the cliff to the right of him.

"If I can get there, I can rest for a while," Steve muttered to himself. He figured his odds of surviving the climb would increase a lot if he could just rest his weary arms, and the thought gave him both renewed hope and a spurt of energy. He focused on finding the easiest path to the opening.

As he got nearer to the cave entrance, he realized that changing direction might have been a critical mistake. He heard the sounds of skeleton warriors below, searching the face of the cliff for him. They spotted him before he reached the cave, and the first arrows began shattering rocks nearby. He sped his pace, spending less time testing crevices and footholds as he scrambled to get to the entrance before one of the arrows found its mark. Just as he finally grasped the ledge that would lead him to safety, an arrow struck just inches from his face. Shards of rock flew into his eyes, blinding him as he heaved himself into the hollow.

Still blind and trying to rub the debris from his eyes,

he stood up. Another arrow whizzed by, grazing Steve's shoulder. He whirled around, disturbing a colony of bats that had been roosting on the roof of the cavern. They flew by Steve, knocking him off balance. He swung his arms wildly and scrambled toward the wall. He realized a moment too late that he'd been turned around and what he thought was a wall was empty space. Recognizing his error and knowing exactly what was going to happen, he nonetheless could not stop himself from stepping into nothingness. He felt his body plummet to the earth and to his death.

Steve flailed his arms and legs on instinct, his mind not realizing that no amount of arm waving would ever get him to fly, or even slow down. What his kicking and flailing did manage to do was give his friend Clem a black eye as the mercenary, and the red dragon he was riding, maneuvered beneath their plummeting friend in an attempt to save his life.

"Ouch!" said the older man. "Stop squirming! We've got you!"

At some point, some part of Steve's brain realized he was no longer falling, and he wasn't dead or even injured. He spun his head around and looked at Clem, who was cradling his eye in his hand. Steve blinked and looked down at Ruby, and only then did he truly understand what had just happened.

"Whoa," he said. "Thanks, guys. Sorry about the eye, Clem."

"What are friends for, dude?"

Steve's wits were slowly coming back to him, and

he remembered the Ender Dragon. "What happened to the other dragon? Did Ruby defeat him?"

"He just flew off," Clem said. "I don't know what happened or why."

Steve slipped the amulet over his head joined his thoughts to Ruby's. He saw the black dragon spew flame, then felt the hatred from its evil, angry mind. Images of dying dragons and burning corpses filled his mind until he had to shut it down for a moment.

Clem looked at him with curiosity in his eyes. Steve shook his head and answered the unasked question. "I just saw, or rather felt, what Ruby saw. The Ender Dragon is one mean, angry beast, but it's not like he doesn't have a reason to hate us."

They were about to land near Hazel and Roger when Steve closed his eyes again and told Ruby to continue. He felt more of the fury of the black dragon fill his mind. While the two dragons battled ferociously, it seemed like neither wanted to hurt the other. What went on behind the fighting was more a battle of minds. The Ender Dragon tried desperately to convince Ruby to join him in his destruction of men while Ruby strove to convince the black dragon to forgive for the sake of both races.

It was the Ender Dragon's last visual message that left Steve stunned. It was a very clear image of a nest full of dragon eggs, awaiting a time when men had been removed from the world. A time when it would be safe for them to hatch.

Steve gasped, "Ruby!" He had felt her need for

dragon companionship ever since he discovered the amulet, and so he knew exactly how much those eggs would mean to her. Even still, she had come back to rescue him. "We are going to help you, Ruby. We're going to get those eggs and make sure you're never alone again."

"What the heck are you talking about, dude?" Clem asked. "What's going on in that head of yours?"

"The Ender Dragon showed her that there were unhatched dragon eggs that he'd been saving for when the world is safe from... us," Steve explained. "He figured that would be the one piece of information that would swing her to his side. When she didn't join him, he left."

"Whoa! No kidding," Clem said as he began climbing off the dragon and onto solid ground. "So maybe the Dragon Master wasn't as crazy as we thought when he was wandering around not collecting dragon eggs."

"Um, no. He was just as crazy as we thought," Steve said as his feet hit the ground as well. "But now we know that there actually are dragon eggs, he'll have a job to do when we've managed to help Ruby find them."

Chapter 23

Once he was off of Ruby, Steve's attention shifted to Chopper. The last time he saw his pet, the poor dog was badly injured. Now, as Steve ran to see his friend, Hazel made way for him. "How is he?" he asked.

"I've given him some healing potion," Hazel replied. "He'll be asleep for a while, but then he'll be as good as new."

Steve breathed a sigh of relief and pulled Chopper toward him. "I was so worried about you," he whispered to the sleeping dog. He looked up and saw his friends looking down and smiling at him. "Thanks for helping him."

It was Clem that replied, "What happened to you, dude? Why were you climbing up?"

Steve was embarrassed that he forgot to mention the army of monsters heading towards them. "Um, I was watching Ruby's battle, with my mind you know, and then a moment later I looked out of the cave and there was a group of skeletons and zombies and who knows what else heading toward the cave. I thought I'd better get out before they arrived, and I wasn't sure how long Ruby would be tied up fighting the Ender Dragon."

Clem asked, "How far away were they?"

"They were right below me when I fell," Steve replied. "I'm surprised you didn't see them. Are we safe up here?"

Hazel shook her head. "We might not be. Roger found a cave entrance just short distance away. If it's connected to the same tunnel system as the lower cave, they could climb up and surprise us."

"Then I suggest we get out of here," Clem said.

Steve saw the problem immediately. "Ruby can only take three of us, plus Chopper. Someone has to be left behind!"

"Why don't we send Roger, Hazel and Chopper back with Ruby," Clem mused. "Then you and I can finish off a few more monsters while we wait for Ruby to come and get us."

Steve felt another tug at his brain. He opened his mind to Ruby and let her share her thoughts.

"Ruby says she can take us all for a short distance. Within walking distance of the nearest village, she thinks." Steve explained. "Why don't we do that, rest for the night, and walk the rest of the way back together. It would give Clem and I a chance to fill you in on everything that's happened."

"Is Ruby sure she can handle the extra weight?" Hazel asked.

"She's sure," Steve said. "But if anyone's got some

food stashed away, she'd like it. She says she's starving."

Clem pulled a few apples out of his pack and tossed them to the dragon. "Sorry Ruby, this is all I've got," he said.

When she was done eating, they worked on getting everyone on board to fly. Chopper was placed in his front basket. Hazel sat directly behind him with Steve squeezed into the seat behind her. Clem took his usual seat, and Roger was left sitting off the saddle, holding on to Clem.

"Hey! Why am I the only one not on the padded seat?" Roger whined.

"You're the only one who has never experienced it before," Clem grinned. "It will be good for you."

"How could it be good for me?" Roger asked.

"You'll better understand what Hazel went through last time she rode a dragon. You'll sympathize more," Clem explained.

"Who is going to sympathize with me?"

"Oh, we all will, Roger," Steve said happily. "Be sure to hang on tight. It's going to be a rough ride!"

Roger reluctantly climbed on and grabbed on to Clem. "I think you guys are enjoying this a bit too much," he complained.

"Let's go, Ruby," Steve called out to the dragon with his voice and mind at the same time.

The great red beast took a few running steps which nearly unseated Roger, then leaped a little less gracefully than usual into the air. Steve almost thought she wouldn't make it, but her powerful wings lifted them all up into the air and toward their destination.

It was a short while later when Ruby landed, again with more difficulty than usual, just outside the nearby town. She was clearly exhausted, and nearly stumbled as she walked through the smooth meadow where they could dismount safely.

Roger, looking rather green, dismounted first. Helped down by Clem, he fell to his back as soon as his feet touched the ground. "I'm never doing that again," he shouted emphatically.

Hazel nimbly hopped down with Chopper in her arms. "The ride was fine. But what is that smell?" She sniffed the air and covered her nose. "It smells like your house before I cleaned up, Roger."

Steve and Clem snickered as they dismounted. Roger huffed and stomped off, trying to regain his dignity.

"It's a strategy we learned that keeps the monsters at bay," Clem told Hazel. "They don't like the smell."

"Neither do I," said Hazel. "But if it keeps people safe, I can deal with it."

Steve told Ruby to hide and rest and promised her that some food would be on its way as soon as they got to the local inn, then they all followed Roger to the center of the village.

CHAPTER 24

In town, the innkeeper remembered Steve and Clem, and seemed a little wary about having them stay again, but after seeing Hazel and Roger with them agreed to give them rooms for the night. He seemed very curious about the ridiculous amount of food ordered by his new guests, but he was happy to provide as long as they could pay.

Steve and Clem went out to the tavern to hear any local gossip. Hazel promised to bring food to Ruby, and Roger decided to take a nap, so he and Chopper remained in the room to sleep.

The tavern was a lively place, and Steve and Clem saw they would have no difficulty finding people to talk to. The bartender gave them each a drink, and they sat down at a table with a group of locals.

"Looks like your wall of garbage is getting pretty big," Clem said. "Is it working to keep the monsters away?"

An old man took a sip of his drink and replied, "Yep, but the garbage smell is starting to reach even the center of town. There's no way to get away from it."

Another man at the table nodded in agreement. "We live near the edge of town, and the smell is horrible," he told Clem. "But at least my family is safe for now."

Steve sniffed the air and understood their issues. "Hopefully, there will be a more permanent and less stinky solution to the monster problem soon," he said. "None of this can last forever."

"Nothin' ever does," said the old man cryptically.

It was then that Hazel came bursting into the room. "Steve! Clem! Hurry! There's something going on. I think the town is under attack!"

Everyone in the tavern stood up and ran toward the door at the same time, causing a bit of a jam. When they managed to sort themselves out, Steve, Clem and Hazel pushed themselves out the door and into the street. Hazel pointed up to where a cloud of arrows was piercing the sky. Not knowing where they were going to come down, Clem yelled out, "Everybody back in!" which caused another crushing jam as everyone tried to run back into the tavern at the same time.

Steve and Clem stayed out and found cover beneath a verandah roof. The arrows landed, mostly harmlessly, just a few meters from where they stood. Steve heard Hazel call out, "Is everyone alright?"

A few calls about dead pigs and chickens rang through, but it appeared there were no other serious injuries.

Steve and Clem remained under cover, waiting for the second round of arrows, but none appeared. Clem shrugged and led Steve out into the street where villagers had already begun clearing the arrows from their homes and yards.

Hazel ran up to them holding an arrow. "They have notes," she called out. "They all have notes attached!"

When she reached them, she pulled out the piece of paper that had been wrapped around the arrow. "They're all the same," she said. "Every single one of them says the same thing."

"What do they say?" Clem asked.

"THIS IS NOT OVER."

Steve and Clem looked at the note. Clem shook his head. "I didn't know skeletons were so into writing."

"They're not," said Hazel. "The Ender Dragon is pretty clearly the mastermind behind this little threat."

"In any case," Steve said, "We need to find that enchanted helmet as soon as possible to stop the nightly attacks," he waved his arms around at the scattered arrows and added, "and this sort of thing."

Getting back to the inn, they found Roger in a heated argument with the innkeeper. "We paid for the night. We're not leaving!" Roger shouted.

"You'll get your money back, but I'm not having you here for a minute longer," the innkeeper howled back. "It's no secret that you're the reason for the attack on the town. I'm not going to let you risk any more lives by staying here!"

It looked as if Roger and the innkeeper were going

to begin a fist-fight before Clem stepped in between them. "Whoa there, dudes!" He turned to the owner of the inn and apologetically said, "My friends and I are very hungry and tired, but we understand how you feel. We signed up for this, you haven't."

"If it was just me," said the innkeeper in a more moderate tone, "I'd let you stay. I'd even fight alongside you. But I've got a whole village of people here to protect, and these folks have been through enough stress and battle with the nightly attacks. They can't deal with more."

Clem nodded his agreement. "We understand. We'll head out shortly." He scribbled short list and handed it to the innkeeper. "If you can pack up six meals to go, and find us these items, we'll pay you for your time, and leave as soon as we can."

The innkeeper nodded, took the list, and headed out the door. Once he was out of the room, Roger turned to Clem. "I thought Ruby couldn't carry us any further! How are we going to leave?"

"She can't carry us," Steve emphatically explained to Clem. "She's exhausted and famished. You haven't felt how tired she is. I have. There's no way..."

Clem waved his hands to interrupt. "I know. When the food comes, arrange for Ruby to meet you. You can give her two of the meals and put Chopper in her saddle," he said to Steve. "She can guard Chopper until they're both recovered. I'm hoping we can find a way to stay behind the garbage defense until morning, but even if we can't, we have to leave. We can't put this entire town at risk any longer."

"What about putting me at risk?" Roger whined. "I don't want to die!"

"Quit complaining," Hazel said as she punched Roger in the arm. "You're safer now than you were in that cave."

Roger rubbed his arm and glared at her, but kept his mouth shut.

When the food came, Steve bundled the still-sleeping Chopper in his arms and headed out to meet Ruby near the edge of the town. Once the two creatures were accommodated, Steve ran back to the inn to help his friends pack.

"There's a fair bit of monster activity out past the garbage defense," Steve told Clem when he returned, "but they seem to be staying pretty far clear of the trash. We'll probably be safe enough if we stay close to the village."

The news cheered the exhausted group as they finished packing their bags and headed out the door.

Chapter 25

Steve's hope that he and his friends could stay within the town's defenses was dashed as they exited the inn. Waiting to escort them out of town was a large group of unhappy villagers holding torches and weapons. He looked at Clem and shrugged as they walked through the crowd toward the town gate.

"What's our next move, mercenary?" Steve asked Clem as they passed the wall of garbage surrounding the town. The last of their villager escort moved back to safety, but stayed within view to make sure their guests were truly leaving.

"We've got a few options. We can start circling the town keeping close to the garbage barrier till sunrise," Clem said thoughtfully. "Or we can take our chances, light up all our torches, and head toward home."

"Which way is home?" Roger asked. "Are we even pointed in the right direction?"

They all turned as they heard a voice yelling at them

from the town. The innkeeper was running their way. Roger looked like he wanted to run away. "Do you think he's mad at us?"

Clem shook his head, "Let's just see what the man has to say."

The man was panting as he came closer. The group waited as he tried to catch his breath. "I couldn't just let you go out there to die without at least trying to help," he said. "I used to have a hunting cabin about a mile that way." He pointed eastward. "I haven't been there since the nightly attacks began. For all I know, it might have been destroyed, but if it's still there it could provide you with enough cover to keep you safe till the sun comes up."

"How do we find it? Clem asked.

"You can't see from here, but if you follow this road for a bit, you'll see a smaller path branching off to the right. Take that, and it will lead you to the field where I kept my cabin." The innkeeper shook his head sadly. "It's not much help, I know, but if you run, it won't take too long to get there."

Clem smiled at the man and clasped his hand to shake it. "Thank you. You've given us a fighting chance at least." He turned to his friends, sizing them up in his mind, and asked, "how fast can you guys run?"

The four companions ran through the woods with Clem at the lead and Steve bringing up the rear. Steve felt frustrated at their slow pace. He knew Clem wasn't even close to going full speed, but was moderating their speed so Hazel and Roger could keep up and not burn out. Even so, Steve felt uneasy in the dark woods and would have liked nothing more than to burst into a sprint.

When he heard a hissing from the woods behind him, he nearly did begin to sprint. Instead he called out Clem's name. When the mercenary turned around, Steve threw him the torch he'd been carrying and pulled out his bow. "Creeper," he said tersely.

Clem nodded and scanned for the source of the noise. "Light an arrow so we can get a better look," he suggested.

When the flaming projectile hit its mark and revealed the terrain behind them, both Steve and Clem muttered curses under their breath. There were dozens of creepers coming at them.

Within seconds, Hazel and Roger were holding all four torches as Steve and Clem let loose a barrage of arrows at the incoming monsters. Explosions shook the forest floor. Steve and Clem stood their ground and continued firing at the creatures. More flaming arrows were interspersed with the standard tips to light up their targets. As they came closer, dirt and debris from the exploding creepers blew back at the companions with every hit.

Steve sent arrow after arrow into the darkness. He shot at every sound and every movement, real and imagined. Even when his arms ached, he didn't dare let up. Even when the explosions became less frequent, he kept firing.

He didn't know how many creatures he'd hit, or how

many arrows he'd sent, but Steve's heart was pounding with adrenaline when Clem finally clamped a hand down on his shoulder and said, "I think we got them, kid."

Letting out a deep breath, Steve lowered his weapon shakily. "I hate creepers," he said. "I really, really hate them."

Clem wordlessly helped him pack his weapon, then gave him one of the torches Roger had been holding. The four of them silently turned back toward their destination and began to run again.

After a few moments, Steve realized that the mercenary had picked up the pace. They were running fast, and he understood why. All the explosions and fire from their battle were sure to attract attention. They had to get out of the area as quickly as possible. He only hoped Hazel and Roger could keep up.

CHAPTER 26

The cabin still had four walls and most of a roof, and Steve was glad for every bit of shelter it gave as he and his friends stumbled past the entrance. Clem did what he could to put the door back in place and prop it up with a few pieces of broken furniture. Steve lit a few wall torches and put a few chairs and a table upright. Hazel was slumped against a wall, breathing heavily, and Roger had collapsed into a heap on the floor.

After making sure Hazel found a seat and a drink, Steve stepped over Roger to stand by the window with Clem. "Anything out there?" he asked the mercenary.

"Nothing yet. Who knows, it might be a quiet night after all."

Hazel interrupted from her seat at the other end of the room, "Clem, why don't you try to get some rest. Steve and I will take the first watch. The night's nearly half over. We'll wake you and Roger up in a few hours, and you can watch while we sleep then."

Clem nodded, grabbed some clothes from his bag to use as a pillow, and curled up in the far corner of the room. Roger had already fallen asleep and was snoring loudly from the patch of floor he'd landed on when he first ran in the door.

Hazel picked up Clem's bow and arrows and walked over to the window to the right of Steve and looked out. A moment later she said softly, "How about filling me in on what I've missed."

Steve took a deep breath, still staring out the window into the darkness. "There's a lot to tell. I'm not sure where to start."

As he began narrating his tale of the Dragon Master, the smelly cabin, the amulet, and his account of the kidnapping and rescue, Hazel listened wide-eyed with amazement. "The Dragon Master is at my house?" she repeated incredulously. "You're sure he's not still crazy? There's a lot of stuff that could get him in trouble there. Potions, traps, enchanted objects - they could all kill him." She punctuated her point by letting an arrow fly at a movement she saw in the woods.

"He's quirky, but pretty sane now," Steve replied. "There's probably a lot you two can talk about. We brought all his books and artifacts with us, too." Steve looked harder out his window and notched an arrow, but didn't see any concerted attack. "In fact, we almost brought everything that didn't stink."

Hazel grinned. "And the garbage barriers work?"

"They seem to," Steve answered. "We had our village start to spread the word about the tactic, so hopefully there are a lot of towns and villages using it to stay safe now."

"Don't tell Roger about it," Hazel said. "He'll think it's a brilliant excuse not to clean up after himself."

Steve chuckled as he swiftly fired two arrows at a pair of skeletons that had just emerged from the deep shadow of the trees. He and Hazel stared intently out their windows, but no further movement drew their fire.

"If you don't want to talk about it, that's okay," Steve said, "but I'd like to hear about how you got captured."

"It was the butcher," Hazel spat. "He was the one who betrayed us."

"Don't worry," Steve said softly. "We'll deal with him when we get back."

"He's already been dealt with," Hazel said. "He ran after our captors as we left town asking for his money. They struck him down and left his body near the side of the road."

"We heard that the guys who kidnapped you were searching your house. Do you know what they were looking for?"

Hazel shook her head. "It wasn't my research that interested them. Maybe they thought I had something related to the armor, but they didn't seem to find whatever they were looking for. Or maybe they weren't even sure what they were after. I think they took a few gold items, but nothing irreplaceable."

"Did you see the Ender Dragon?"

"Not till you and Ruby showed up," Hazel said. "Was

the dragon at the village too?"

"I hate to tell you this, but Roger's house has been demolished. The blacksmith said he saw a dragon hit it with a fireball."

Hazel muttered a curse under her breath. "I had some really helpful books in that house." She fired off several arrows into the darkness. Steve wasn't sure if she was aiming at anything or just letting off steam, but he strained his eyes searching the shadows for movement while he let Hazel work out her anger in silence.

Some time had passed before she spoke again. "I think it's about time we woke up Clem and got some rest ourselves."

Steve nodded and stepped over to where Clem was sleeping. He gave the mercenary a nudge, and immediately Clem was awake and alert.

"Everything okay, dude?"

"Yeah. I hope you had a good rest," Steve told him. It's been pretty quiet out there, but it's your turn to take watch."

Steve watched as Hazel found herself a place to rest, then he lay on his back with his head on Clem's pile of clothes and promptly fell asleep.

Chapter 27

Steve groaned as Clem shook him awake. He felt as if he'd just fallen asleep a moment ago, but between his squinted eyelids he saw that the sun was beginning to peek out over the horizon. He rubbed his eyes and tried to get the cobwebs out of his brain.

"Time to get moving, dude," Clem said cheerfully. "Roger and I have packed up everything but the clothes you're using as a pillow."

Steve looked up to see the bags all packed, but some food left out for Hazel and him on the table. He groaned again and forced his body up and off the floor. "I really need one good night's sleep."

"Don't we all," said Clem. "But today's not the day for that. Get some food in your stomach and let Ruby know we're leaving. We'll walk from here to give her a break. In any case, it's time to go home." Clem looked at Roger apologetically. "Well, back to whatever's left of home for some of us."

Steve opened his mind to Ruby and let her know they were hiking out of the forest to Hazel's cottage. Ruby surprised him by suggesting she could fly them all, as long as they stopped halfway for a big meal and short rest.

When Steve told the others, the reaction was mixed. Hazel was delighted. Clem was worried she was taking on too much. Roger shook his head and said he'd rather walk. Steve questioned Ruby again to make sure that's what she wanted, and the dragon was adamant that she could do it.

"Okay, we're flying folks. We can meet Ruby in the clearing by the path we came here on," Steve said. "Since we're not walking, we won't be needing most of the leftover food. Ruby can have it when we rest."

In no time at all, they were soaring high above the trees. Ruby was slowed down by their weight; Steve knew, but the landscape below flew by quickly, and they made incredible time. It was less than an hour later that the dragon decided to land and rest for a while.

Roger fell off Ruby's back looking a little green. He grabbed hold of a tree for support and spent a few minutes recuperating before he managed to speak. "Are we halfway already? Maybe we could walk from here."

Steve was about to deny the request outright when Clem said, "You know, Roger and I could walk it together. The road is pretty straight and flat from here to Hazel's, and if Ruby needs to rest for another hour or more, we might even make it there about the same time as you."

Roger beamed. "Yes! Let's do that!"

Steve shrugged. He figured Clem was just offering to make Ruby's last trip less arduous, and he was grateful. Since it was still morning there wouldn't be too much danger facing them on foot, even if it took them an extra few hours.

"Be sure to take a bit of food and a lot of water with you," he told them. "If you're not there an hour after we arrive, we'll send Ruby out to find you."

Roger looked horrified. "We'll be there!" he said emphatically. "I guarantee it." He grabbed Clem's arm and pulled him toward the road. "Let's get moving, Clem!"

Clem laughed and fell into a brisk walk beside Roger. "See you later!" he called out, waving to his friends.

Hazel and Steve sat down under a tree and watched Chopper as he played in a small stream nearby. Ruby was fast asleep. The sun and the breeze made Steve feel the effects of sleep deprivation even more than usual. "Do you mind if I snooze for a while too?" he asked Hazel.

"Not at all," she replied. "A little solitude is just what I need right now. I'll keep watch."

With that, Steve rested his head against the tree trunk and joined Ruby in a dreamland where dragons filled the skies.

When he awoke, he was completely refreshed. "How

long did I sleep?" he asked Hazel. "I feel amazing."

"A few hours," she replied. "Ruby just woke up too."

He looked over at the red dragon who was leisurely stretching her massive body. "Looks like she's feeling better too," Steve said with a grin. "I guess we're both ready to go again."

They climbed on to the oversized saddle, and secured Chopper on the front, and with effortless grace, Ruby launched herself into the air.

Hazel laughed. "This is wonderful!" she called out to Steve.

Steve realized that this was the first time she'd had the opportunity to experience Ruby at her finest. They'd ridden without a saddle before, but that was not an experience she would remember fondly. Clem's saddle offered stability and comfort that let her enjoy the experience rather than just trying to survive it, and without the extra weight Ruby was soaring fast and joyously.

It wasn't long before Steve saw Roger and Clem walking on the road below them. They'd had a long head-start, but Ruby was flying at full speed. Rather than pointing out their friends on foot, Steve mentally asked the dragon to do a low flyover so they could wave. Ruby tipped into a dive that had Hazel laughing with pleasure. When she saw Roger and Clem, she called out and waved furiously.

Steve waved too. He was grinning broadly at Hazel's delight. She had been through a lot, Steve thought. If anyone deserved a few moments of pure happiness, it was Hazel.

Ruby swooped back up into the sky, and they continued their flight toward Hazel's cabin.

Chapter 28

As they came to a landing near the cabin, Ladon burst out of the house and ran toward them. Steve couldn't help but grin. This introduction should be entertaining. He was a little disappointed that Clem wouldn't be here to witness it.

Steve helped Chopper out of his compartment and then slid off the saddle himself before turning to help Hazel come down off of Ruby's back. By the time they had all dismounted, Ladon was standing right beside them, bouncing up and down with excitement.

"Steve! Clem? Hey! Where's Clem? Is he okay? The red dragon! Can I talk to her? Can I have the amulet?" Ladon was speaking in a fast staccato that momentarily overwhelmed Steve. "You must be Hazel," the Dragon Master continued, grabbing Hazel's hand and shaking it vigorously. "I've learned so much about you from your home. Oh no! I'm sorry. I shouldn't have snooped. I didn't even ask permission to be here! Please don't be mad!"

Steve put both hands on Ladon's shoulders. "Calm down," he said in a soft voice. "Clem's fine, and I told Hazel you would be here. Everything's good."

The old man stopped speaking though he still seemed to be bouncing in place.

"It's nice to meet you, Ladon," Hazel said in a soothing voice. "I'm sure we'll have a lot to talk about. Let's get Ruby settled, and we'll all go inside and chat."

Steve handed Ladon the amulet, hoping a quick conversation with Ruby would mellow the old man out a little bit. With Hazel helping it took only a few minutes to remove the packs and saddle from the dragon's back.

When Hazel went into the cabin to bring out food for Ruby and Chopper, Steve took a moment to watch the Dragon Master. He looked much cleaner, and better fed, than he had when Clem and Steve had left him at the cabin. The old man was sitting cross-legged on the ground, apparently communicating with the dragon. He had a huge grin on his face. Steve couldn't help but smile at the sight.

Steve was about to turn around when Ladon noticed him staring. The old man gave Ruby a hug and ran back to Steve as the dragon went to eat the food Hazel had prepared. "Ruby is so amazing!" Ladon exclaimed as he handed back the amulet to Steve.

"Yeah, she sure is," Steve replied. "Why don't we all go back inside. I think you and Hazel will have a lot to talk about."

"I know," the Dragon Master said excitedly. "She's got some excellent books, and her research is incredible!"

Steve was initially glad to see that he was correct in his guess that Hazel and Ladon would have a lot to discuss. They talked, and talked, and Steve understood very little of what they were saying. It didn't take long before he grew bored and restless. He decided to head outside to chat with Ruby.

Ruby, as it turned out, was anxious to talk to him too. No sooner had he stepped into her view than she projected an image into his mind. The eggs the Ender Dragon had shown her were on her mind. She made it clear to Steve that she wanted to search for them as soon as possible.

Steve sympathized with her but tried to explain that it was important that they find the diamond helmet first.

Ruby was insistent and projected the image of the eggs to him again.

Steve stressed that the helmet was more important, and told her that the world wouldn't be safe for baby dragons until it had been found.

Ruby sent him the image of the eggs once again.

Steve was feeling a little bit frustrated. He was about to insist on the importance of the helmet when he felt Ruby push his focus to a spot in between the eggs.

"What is it, Ruby?" Steve said out loud. "Is there something wrong with that egg?"

As the image in his mind focused even more, he felt like an idiot. Could it be? "The helmet?" He asked out loud. Ruby communicated an affirmative answer. The enchanted helmet was hidden among the dragon eggs. "Well, then I guess we're going after both at once," he said sheepishly.

Steve was still red with embarrassment when he heard Clem and Roger calling from the path below. Steve called back, "Hey! What took you guys so long?"

"Roger wanted to check on his house before we came," Clem replied.

"It's utterly destroyed!" Roger complained.

"Quit whining, Roger," Clem said. "We've got the townsfolk all helping to rebuild."

"Think of it this way, Roger," Steve said. "At least now you don't have to clean up your junk from the living room!"

Clem laughed while Roger pouted.

Steve joined them as they entered Hazel's cabin. "Roger, meet Ladon. He's a Dragon Master."

Roger turned to Ladon and smiled his best salesman smile. "Hello. I'm pleased to meet you. Would you like to buy this lovely bush for three diamonds?"

Ladon looked over at Clem and Steve with a bewildered look on his face. When he saw they were stifling their laughter, he grinned back at Roger. The Dragon Master ran to the wall near the cot he'd been sleeping on and grabbed something from the floor. "I don't have diamonds," he said as he held out the object. "But I'll trade you the bush for this dragon egg."

"But that's just a rock!" Roger exclaimed.

"And your bush is very dead."

Roger pondered this for a moment, then nodded, and the two swapped the useless items.

At this, Steve and Clem could no long hold in their laughter. Steve doubled over while Clem was reduced to rolling around on the floor.

If Roger picked up on the joke, he certainly never let on. He looked at the two laughing men critically. "I don't know why you said I'd have a lot in common with Ladon," he said. "He's nothing like me!"

About the Author

David H. Scott was born in 2002 in Ontario, Canada. He enjoys writing, gaming, modding Minecraft and developing video games. He thinks the 12th Doctor is superlative, and *The Force Awakens* is the best Star Wars movie.

He loves to read middle grade and young adult novels, he's a practitioner of several martial arts, and to keep coin in his pocket (until he becomes a rich and famous novelist) he delivers newspapers.

The Lost is his second novel, and the second book in the Tales of the Ablockalypse trilogy.

You can find out more about David's books at http://mysticawesome.com/

CPSIA information can be obtained at www.ICGtesting.com
Printed in the USA
LVOW10s0546220316

480217LV00009B/40/P